OVER THE EDGE

The Edge - Book Four

CD REISS

If any person or event in this book seems too real to be true, it's luck, happy coincidence, or wish-fulfillment on the reader's part.

AUTHOR'S NOTE: I did research. A ton of it. But I also make stuff up for a living.

There are a thousand ways to break something and more than one method of repair. Institutions we think we know from experience have engaged thousands of others in their own, equally valid experiences. What you assume is an error may be something else entirely. Or I might have fucked up.

You can poke me with corrections on any number of subjects and if I can fix an error, I will. I'm wrong a lot.

Also, liberties were taken.

❀ Created with Vellum

Part One

TENSION

Chapter One

THE GREEN ZONE
FIVE DAYS AFTER GREYSON TAKES BICAM

I kept my promises. Every one of them. To my country. To the military. To my wife. But I never realized how easy it had been. Greyson would have called my life a cakewalk. That was her word. Cakewalk. When my world was gray and flat, she spoke in full color. I missed her. She was in the room with me, but I missed her.

Knock-knock.

My not-wife sat on the edge of a worn chair in her apartment, looking into the space between the imaginary horizon and the deepest part of her soul, filtering details through a wider and wider net. With the knock, she shut her mouth tight and looked to me for her next move.

Greyson never would have looked to me for guidance. Not that flatly. Not without having an opinion written all over her face.

"Wait here," I said.

"Yes."

I opened the door and… as expected… it was Ronin with a box under one arm. He had a puppy dog look, and even though I'd never been a fan of the sneaky bastard, at least I'd always known exactly what kind of sneaky bastard I was dealing with.

Not anymore. Now I had no idea who he was or what he wanted.

I came out and closed the door behind me before I reached for the box.

He stepped back. "No."

"No? What the fuck did you come here for then?"

"We should talk. All of us."

"All five of us?" I went for the box, but he twisted away.

"I want to see her."

"Why?"

"I want to make sure she's all right." He swallowed hard, glancing at the door, then back at me. "This stuff, it fucks with you."

"Tell me about it."

"Just one second," he said expectantly. "Then I'll go."

"Jesus, I bet you were a nice kid before the army fucked you up."

From the other side of the door, her shriek split the night. "Let me *go*!"

Chapter Two

GREYSON

MINUTES AFTER THE SHOT

Never take anything for granted.

Anything.

When a piece of metal had missed my heart by a fraction of the length of my fingernail, I'd stopped taking my safety for granted, adding that to my overall health and the health of my family. I never took Caden's love for granted, nor his well-being. Never money. Never my friends.

But I'd taken my sanity for granted. I'd leaned on it as the one thing I could always count on, no matter what. My mental stability was the rock I'd lashed the rest of myself onto as the earth shook and the winds tried to rip me away.

I was sane. My perceptions were keen and clear. My personality was steady, clearly defined as *me*, and with that collateral in my pocket, I could risk everything else.

It couldn't be bartered, spent, or worn away. I could not be disengaged from it. My very existence had been poured into the vessel of my sanity.

Even after seeing Caden fall apart, I'd depended on that container to hold me together, assuming it was indestructible.

When I took the shot meant for my husband, the assumption remained. It was a placebo...or not. If it was, I'd be fine. If it wasn't, then I'd still be me, no matter what I'd injected into myself. No vial of experimental serum could take away the essentialness of *me* because that was where the unmovable object and the unstoppable force met. It was the only real thing in the world.

"Why did you do that?" Caden asked outside the hospital.

My arm throbbed at the injection site. I hadn't been careful with the needle, nor had I stuck it into thick-enough muscle.

"I don't trust him." I said, knowing Caden would understand I was talking about Ronin. "What happened to Yarrow, I don't want it to happen to you. And if I wouldn't give you the shot, Dana would."

He took me in his arms, and there the splitting sky was sewn shut. I thought I was just tired. A little stressed out. All I needed was a good night's sleep and Caden St. John.

"Why?" he asked. "Why not just dump it if you didn't want me to have it?"

"The syringe had a tell. If it didn't go into someone, they would have known."

"So what?"

"They'd just send more, and if I wouldn't give it to you, someone else would." There was more to it than that, of course. If I'd dumped it, another solution would have presented itself in time. But I took my sanity for granted, so I'd gone with the solution I had on hand because it would satisfy my need to save Caden.

"I had to know if it was a placebo or not," I said. "If I tossed it, we'd never know."

"Well?" He laid a kiss on my cheek. "Is it?"

His question wasn't urgent. He wasn't worried or uneasy, because he took my sanity for granted as well.

"Not sure," I said even though I was very sure something had shifted. I laid my lips on the bare bit of skin over his collar, breathing deeply of coffee grounds and lingering rubbing alcohol. The scent went from my nose, down my spine, between my legs, where it burst into a throb that beat with my heart. "Maybe it was an aphrodisiac."

"I'm off duty at oh four hundred," he said.

"Can you get to my apartment at that hour?"

"Probably. The army never sleeps."

Dropping my arms away from him, I stepped back. I felt the sky rip into two halves—two eyes watching me from deep in the past—and still thought I had it under control. I could watch the effects of the drug like a clinician and let them wear off like a person with a deep well of sanity.

"Be there," I said.

"Be naked," he replied with a smirk.

He took two steps backward to the hospital, turning when the doors *whoosh*ed open. I watched him walk away, yanking the tether between us tight, tighter, near breaking but not quite.

Not yet.

Maybe I took that for granted too.

I'D TAKEN the shot instead of wasting it because I didn't want Blackthorne to know it didn't go into Caden. Once I realized Caden's syringe hadn't been filled with a placebo, I got pissed off. That was not okay. Not for Caden. Not for anyone.

At 02:23:00, the Blackthorne offices were dark and empty. I sat at my desk and dashed off an email I was pretty sure I'd regret.

FROM: GFrazier@blackthorne.com
TO: RBlake@blackthorne.com
CC: DGionetto@blackthorne.com

RONIN:

Dana has logged subject Dr. Caden St. John's vial as administered because the syringe corroborates and because I told her it was.

This email is to correct the record. The dose was administered to me. The subject was the only witness. Dana is not at fault for the erroneous log. I will submit corrected paperwork first thing in the morning.

As an aside, the syringe did not contain a placebo. I

am experiencing noticeable symptoms of scopaesthesia. As these syringes do not contain what I—the accountable physician—was told is in them, I will no longer be administering BiCam, nor will I sign off on the administration of BiCam by any physician's assistant under my purview.

Best regards,

Dr. Greyson Frazier

PS: Fuck you.

I DELETED the postscript before I sent it. He needed to hear that to his face.

When I shut the computer down, my eyes needed a moment to adjust.

Medical books. Binders. A chair and a couch. An open door looking onto a large room with rows of desks facing north to minimize the sun's glare. My office had a window that looked out onto that wider room. Blinds shut.

The shut blinds bothered me. I kept them that way to protect the privacy of whomever was in the room with me. The door was open unless I was seeing someone or on a call. Normal.

But something was behind those blinds.

There was no noise. No visual. No sense other than a conviction I knew was wrong. I could see the large room through the door, and it was dead-of-night empty. If someone had come in, I would have heard the outer door.

Foolish, of course. I was just jumpy from the dark and years of fighting an enemy who could be anywhere. This wasn't the same thing Caden had experienced. It was manageable because I was in complete control of my mind.

I reached for cold common sense and felt the rip in the sky again. The bowl over all of us cracking in two and becoming sentient. Potential energy turned kinetic. Death turning to life.

I was tired, and it had been a stressful day. After gathering my things, I went to the doorway and paused before going through. Quietly, I leaned over and twisted the rod that opened the blinds and jumped at the sight of a shadow. I went back into the office and shut the door. Locked it. Jerking the cord at the side of the window, I raised the blinds.

The shadow was a coat hanging on a hook.

"For fuck's sake," I said to myself. My voice was a balm against the shifting reality, filling the crack like epoxy. "Just go home already."

BLACKTHORNE HAD a shuttle bus that ran between the office and the apartments all day and night. One was waiting outside for me. I chatted with the driver. The wheels moving under my feet felt right and good. I was moving. Going someplace. Forward momentum was exactly what I needed, and by the time I walked into my apartment at almost three in the morning, I felt normal again.

Caden might be hungry, and after he fucked me, I might feed him. I cut oranges and a stubby banana. Brewed mint tea and set out crackers. Then I stripped to bare skin and showered.

The injection site looked normal. The tiny pinprick would fade to nothing in a day.

For the first time, I considered that I might get fired for my impulse. I *should* get fired and sent home. Being separated from Caden would be the worst consequence, but maybe I'd done what I came here to do...save him from that shot. Maybe I could go home and just wait for his return, knowing I hadn't come to Iraq for nothing.

The idea of going home was like walking backward.

I paced naked to the opposite side of the studio apartment.

There couldn't be a backward. Stillness was death. There was only forward.

I couldn't go home.

A light rap at the door. I shut off the lights. I jumped onto the bed as he let himself in, a tall shadow against the outside lights. Like an animal, I could sense his scent and his energy. When he closed the door, I leapt off the bed, unable to sit still, and pushed him against the door.

We were open mouths and searching tongues. I was made of hands that opened, peeled, shucked his clothes away until the hard heat of his cock was in my hands.

Forward. Forward. Forward.

He pushed me to my knees, and I took him in my mouth, flattening my tongue against his shaft, opening my throat so he could push forward, always forward. He growled and took me by the hair, jerking my face off his spit-slick cock, looking down at me with eyes lit from within.

"I'm going to eat you alive," he said, pulling me up.

"I thought you might be hungry."

He pushed me onto the couch. "Up on your knees."

I kneeled on the cushions, facing him. He sat on the floor with his back to the couch and bent his neck upward, reaching back to draw my wet cunt over his face. His tongue prodded into me, then found my clit, flicking it. His legs made a V on the carpet, and his erect cock added a third dimension to the shape. Up and out. Sucking my clit, licking it gently, and sucking again. I needed to be on his dick's trajectory. That shaft was desire. It was want. It was the shape of our need. Up, over, beyond, and if I could harness it, I'd be shot through the crack in the sky.

I rode his face as if I wanted to drive over the speed limit. Open this baby up. See how fast we could go. His hands wrapped around my legs, gripping the tops of my thighs tightly as if he could control my heat.

"Yes," I moaned. "More. More."

I came, driving my pelvis against his face, reaching my arms to the ceiling, exploding in all directions except the one I needed.

Forward.

Without taking an extra breath, I crawled off the couch, put my feet on either side of his hips and my hands on his thighs.

"Whoa, baby," he said from behind me. "Give

yourself—"

I impaled my body on his cock, driving down the full length of him.

"God damn," he muttered in wonderment.

I pulled up and slammed back down again.

"Fuck it, baby." He balled my hair in his fist again, yanking my head around so I could see him. He was a king dressed in the raiment of my body. "Fuck it hard. Work for it."

I lifted and fell again and again, speeding up but never going shallow. I wished I was deeper. I wished he was longer. I wished we could go deep and through and come out the other side. But as fast as I went and as deep as I pushed, the boundaries between us only became more frustratingly clear.

"Hang on," he said, but I ignored him.

I wouldn't be stopped or slowed. Moderation didn't find the limit. Safety didn't tease out the edges.

Caden twisted me off him and flipped me to my stomach. I grunted in protest. I didn't want to be passive. I didn't want to be ridden. I wanted to ride.

He was inside me before I could explain, so deep I thought he'd crack me.

"Is this what you want?" he asked.

"Deeper."

He got on his knees, pulling me up until I was crouched over him. We were both facing the same direction, and that seemed more right than anything before. Reaching under me, he spread my thighs apart and angled his cock to my entrance.

"Fuck it. Put all your weight on it."

I pushed down as hard as I could. He wrapped his arms around me and thrust his hips up.

"Yes," I said. "All the way. All of you inside me."

His fingers found my clit and circled it. There was no more thrusting, only pushing deeper until I felt him in my gut, hurting me with desire. Into. Forward. Through. Facing the same direction together.

I came from the bottom of my lungs. I came from the tip of his cock to the vibrations in my throat with a long *nnnn* sound that rattled every nerve in my body.

Not quite finished, I sucked in a breath like a drowning woman, and he pushed me off him, bent me over the couch, and reentered me. Putting his weight between my shoulder blades, he held me still, taking me from behind as though he owned me, asking for nothing but his own pleasure. He drove into me as if my body didn't have a limit.

"—come inside you," he said breathlessly. "Take it deep."

He found an untouched depth. An arcane secret in my belly that I'd been holding for him and only him. When he discovered it, he hurt me and broke through to another orgasm. It emerged with renewed velocity, bursting to the surface like a diver breaking through the water.

I shook. Or the earth quaked. Or reality trembled, threatening to break and spill its contents. It managed to hold together. For now.

HE'D EXHAUSTED me so much that even when I slept, I was awake, and when I woke, I was still asleep. I spun down a tunnel that was focused and clear in the center but more and more chaotic at the edges.

"No fever." Caden's voice, like the details of my world, was crisp and lucid as I heard it and fractured and shattered as it drew away, like a Doppler effect of cognizance. "Take this for the headache."

When I sat up to take the ibuprofen, the tunnel moved a little behind me, bending from inertia and snapping into place after a second.

"Did I tell you I had a headache?"

I was starting to doubt the words that came out of my mouth.

"I know when your head hurts, sweetheart."

I handed him back the glass. "Thank you."

"You don't look good," he said. "Are you going to be okay?"

I nodded, and the tunnel shook, waving lucidity before me like a red cape. When he kissed me, my consciousness shifted to where his lips touched my skin, and his voice was the focal point of my attention.

He laid my head on the pillow and covered me, promising he'd return as soon as he could. I barely heard him. My temperature was normal, but I was in a fevered half dream. The dashing thoughts repeated over and over like a mantra, falling into dissonance, only to echo as if I'd lost control of my inner voice.

At one point, between sleep and wakefulness, the bed seemed to drop from under me and the blankets hovered a few inches above.

Not really. I checked by laying my hand on the mattress and pressing down. But once I closed my eyes again, I hovered in space.

Not quite falling. Not quite flying. Stopped in time.

Cool air hit my face and my flailing limbs. It drove itself between my panties and my skin, making me aware of the angle of my body and the fact that no matter how much I flapped my arms, I couldn't will myself to fly.

I could still feel where he'd touched me. Where he'd violated me with his finger as if my body was his. The curdled nerves inside my vaginal wall were disgusted and greedy for more. One side of my bra was hitched over a nipple, hard from the damp and cold, and my lips were wet from inexpert kisses.

I'd escaped something but not what I'd always thought. Maybe rape but not rape. I'd escaped something I couldn't define.

Twisting, I could see the sky over the UCLA diving pool. The stars were cut out in the shape of Scott's perfect body perched on the edge of the platform, his knees bent to propel himself after me. The crescent of the moon looked as if it was balanced on my big toe, as if I'd cut half a glowing nail and hadn't ripped it away yet. The pool's filter churned like a diesel engine, and the mating song of the crickets that lived under the bushes on the other side of the fence was louder than an electric guitar.

Falls were survivable. Falls into a pool especially so. But doing it wrong hurt, and in my expanded airborne second and a half, I straightened as much as I could, watching the turquoise rectangle of the pool hurtle toward me. I closed my eyes. The wet touch of the surface hit my shoulder, and the cool air from it blew against my cheek for the shortest of split seconds in the elastic perception of time.

When I held my breath, time snapped back. My ears filled with the *whoosh* of bubbles. Pain shot through my shoulder when I tried to swim up. With a second *whoosh*, Scott broke the surface like a spear and scooped me up, pulling me to the surface.

I'd survived something.

I didn't know what, but I'd endured more than falling from the diving platform.

When Scott got me to the edge of the pool and I tried to grab the lip with my bad arm, I cried, "Ow."

"What were you trying to do?" he asked, getting out in one move like he did a hundred times a day.

His question was pure accusation, as if I'd done something crazy. He didn't know my collarbone was broken. He didn't know I was hurt, and I didn't either. I couldn't lift my arm, and I didn't care. I could hold on with the other one.

I was happy.

So happy I couldn't wipe the smile from my face.

Scott stood over me with his hand out, scowling, his body covered in dripping diamonds.

The happiness overtook me so hard I laughed in pure delight. Not because I was alive.

No.

I was overjoyed at the sight of the boy standing over me.

For reasons I couldn't explain in the halfway point between sleep and wakefulness, with my perceptions distorting at the edges, I was relieved that Scott was alive.

"Why did you jump?" he asked, truly concerned. He'd put his hands where they didn't go and scared me, but he wasn't a bad person. He was salvageable, and so was I.

My unreasonable joy grew like a water balloon stuck to a flowing hose. By jumping, I'd saved him.

I didn't know why I thought that, and I was afraid I was going to find out.

Chapter Three

CADEN

Even asymmetrical war has a pattern. Days of nothing led into a barrage of casualties that lasted days about one third of the time. The other two-thirds were one-off IEDs or suicide bombers in crowded markets. Not fun. Every soldier who came in shaken to their core was proof that the system was broken, and every single hurt civilian convinced me it had to end.

But I had my detachment. I could still compartmentalize. Choosing it instead of having it thrust upon me brought a relieved kind of euphoria.

"She's going to kill me," the corporal said as the nurse, a petite brunette with freckles, used a ring cutter to get his wedding band off his broken hand.

"She's going to be happy you're alive. Look up." I shined a light in his eye. The cornea had been scratched by a flying pebble.

"Am I going blind?" he asked as Bones pressed his freed knuckle. "Ow! *Fuck*!"

"You just bought yourself a ticket to Germany," the orthopedist said.

"Have a beer for me," I added before turning to the freckled nurse. "Can you get me an eye dressing?"

DeLeon poked her head in. "Eyes."

"Just the left," I said, cleaning out the corporal's orbital cavity.

"No, *Dr.* Eyes." Recently, for reasons I couldn't get to the bottom of, she'd stripped the Asshole off my name. "Got a guy here to see you."

"I'm busy."

"Well, then." Her voice turned a little sultry. I looked around to see if she was directing it at me. "I'll have to wait with him then."

"Whatever."

"Take your time," she replied with a wink.

RONIN AND DELEON were chatting in one of the waiting areas when I came out. There was a match made in hell for sure.

We shed my CO and went to a deserted corner of the chow hall patio.

"Sorry to pull you into a corner," he said.

"No problem. I love the cloak-and-dagger shit."

"We need to talk about what Greyson did last night."

"Do we?" I got immense pleasure from giving him a hard time.

"Did she tell you why she took the shot?"

"No." I blew on my coffee, considering the sanctity of marital privilege. "Why don't you ask her?"

"She's not in the office today, and she doesn't answer the phone, her email, or the fucking door."

"I'm sure she'll fill out a report or whatever you people do."

"I want to hear it from you."

"Really?" I sipped my coffee. I was taking it with less and less sugar these days. The sweetness seemed like a lie against the backdrop of ripped bone and flesh.

"Did you tell her to take it?"

The idea was so hilarious I nearly spit my coffee.

"What's so funny?"

"Have you met my wife?" Putting the cup down, I leaned back. "Can you imagine her doing anything I tell her just because I said so?"

He shook his head and looked into his coffee. "She didn't want to give it to you. She was afraid you'd react. She thought it might not be a placebo."

"Bad researcher," I scolded. "You're not supposed to tip your hand to the patient."

"Done is done. You're out of the study. Which is too bad. You were good."

"It didn't feel good."

"Trust me. You were great." He leaned his elbows on the table, circling his cup with his palms. "I never saw anything like you in Fallujah."

My cup froze halfway to my lips.

In Fallujah?

I observed Ronin only to find he was observing my reaction just as carefully.

I put down my coffee. "Is there something you want to tell me?"

"You should ask your wife."

He wasn't sitting that far away. If I stood, I could reach across the table and grab the collar of his Blackthorne polo before I punched him in the face. The coffee would spill. I might get arrested if he didn't beat the shit out of me first. A small price to pay for the implication that Greyson hid things from me.

"Here's the problem," he said, lowering his voice. Good strategy. In order to hear him, I had to pay more attention, which drained my anger of its explosiveness. "I don't know what was in the shot."

"How is that possible?" I growled.

He was fucking with my wife now. He could take his *soo-hoo*s and his benchmark tests and shove them. I didn't care what he did with me. I'd volunteered for that shit. But Greyson? Fucking with her wasn't okay. I must have looked like a wild animal because he went fake beta on me, averting his eyes and relaxing his shoulders as if he had no intention of attacking. Not physically.

"It's a big business," he said. "Blackthorne. If you count overseas income streams, it's bigger than AT&T."

"And?"

"And that means there are a lot of people. You just see me. That's by design. But my bosses have bosses, and there are parts of this program that are out of my control. We got those syringes sealed, with names and serial numbers already on them. We recommended a placebo as a control, but"—he shrugged—"I don't know."

One, two, three deep breaths. I said nothing.

"They're motivated to get this process to work," he continued. "As long as there's no childhood trauma, the shot plus the breathing has a two-pronged effect. It improves combat performance and releases the burden of battle distress. It's a win all around. But there's an actuarial component to this. Sometimes things are going to go to shit. The wrong people are going to get it, or a mistake in dosage will have side effects. The bean counters need to know what that's going to cost them."

"And the only way is to get it wrong and see what it costs."

"Right."

"What is that shit?"

"Does it matter?"

"Yes."

He pushed his coffee away and put a napkin in front of him. After slipping a pen from his pocket, he clicked it and drew on the napkin. Lines. Letters. A chemical compound.

"This is proprietary," he said, connecting lines and tucking abbreviations into the corners. "I could get sued into the poorhouse."

The chain of elements went on and on.

"I'm not a chemist," I said.

"I'm betting on that."

"I don't need you to prove a point."

He kept scribbling his molecule, opening the napkin to make more room. "The circular breathing's important. BiCam, the stuff we were working with in Fallujah? It was a breakthrough. But the army didn't want to hear anything from me. Not after Abu Ghraib." A short rip appeared where he pressed too hard. "I got busted down to Aberdeen piss boy after that."

He pushed the napkin toward me.

"Like I told you," I said, "I'm not a chemist. What does this have to do with Greyson?"

He took the napkin and crunched it into a ball.

"Dose and preparation." He took a Zippo and a pack of Marlboros from his pocket and poked out a smoke. "It's highly personalized." He bit the cigarette out of the pack and lit it, keeping the lighter open. "Your dose was raised over time."

He set the napkin on fire.

"The shots in New York weren't vitamins." I stated it as a fact because it was. I didn't need confirmation.

"Sure, they were. With more or less BiCam depending." He dropped the flaming ball on the table. "We were making you into a god. The split was going to be managed with bioenergetic breathing once you had the sessions under control. But the army brought you here and cut me out. So, I hired Greyson because she'd watch you until I could get transferred." A line of hot orange sped to the center of the napkin, and the black edges curled and flaked off. "Now she's taken your dose."

"Which is higher because I'm acclimated. And you have no idea what effect it's going to have on her."

"And here we are."

The last of the napkin turned to cold carbon. A ribbon of smoke curled between us and went dead.

"I know you're covered legally." I flicked away the black ash. "I know what I signed. I can only imagine what my wife had to sign to come here. So, when I say this, I want you to take it personally. This isn't about the law or military channels. This is about you and me. Nothing else. No one else. If she's damaged in any way, I'm coming after you. You're going to wish you were a piss boy."

He jammed his cigarette between his teeth and smiled around it as if relishing the challenge.

"Until then," he said around his smoke, "you need me."

THE APARTMENT WAS SO dark and still I thought she'd left. I turned on a lamp and shut the door. She was on the bed in the same position I'd left her, on her side, left foot poking from under the covers. When I took her hair off her face, her eyes were closed and she was smiling.

"Hey, baby."

Her lids fluttered, and she refocused. "Hey."

"How are you feeling?"

"All right."

"You haven't moved."

She got up on an elbow and looked around. The fruit from the night before had collected tiny flies, and her clothes were still on the floor. "I guess I haven't."

I ran my fingers over her forehead, the worst way to check for fever, but I didn't want to go full medical professional on her just yet. Her voice had a tenderness I didn't want to disrupt.

"Are you hungry?" I touched her lower lip. It was swollen from sleep, yielding and soft.

"I don't think so."

The sheet slid down her body, revealing the peaks of her breasts. I ran two fingers from her lip, down her chin, over the hardening nubs. She smiled again, looking down at my hand. Her dark lashes fanned out against her cheeks, fluttering as I moved the sheet below her waist.

"What do you want?" I asked, feeling the depth of the crease between her thighs. She gave no more than what the force of my touch demanded.

"Whatever you want."

"Open your legs."

She spread her knees apart. I ran my hand inside her thighs, brushing her outer lips. She closed her eyes, releasing a gentle gasp. When I pushed her legs apart, she threw her head back, exposing the length of her throat.

"I talked to Ronin today." I slid my finger in her seam, teasing it open. "You told him you were having symptoms?"

"It's not that bad. I think it'll go away." She looked at me, spreading wider.

"What symptoms?"

She rocked her legs back and forth, teasing me with the sight of her pussy.

"Feeling watched. But I know it's not true, so I think I'll get it under control."

She'd seen me break in two, yet she thought her symptoms would just go away because she knew the cause. Was it ego or confidence? I admired her stability and strength, but I wasn't imprudent enough to depend on them. I knew what this shit did to a person. I'd been like this before Damon peeled away and became his own man. Confident. Cocky. Foolish.

"I'm still pissed at Ronin," she said.

"He told me what they were trying to do."

She faced forward, looking at me but... not quite. Her gaze was slightly averted.

"Make warriors?" she said with a question at the end. "I didn't know. I still don't really know."

"I need to know how you're feeling. I need to know if it's hurting you."

"I feel fine," she said. "A little run-down. But fine."

I believed her. I trusted that she knew her own mind because I wanted to. Her clit was hot and wet on the backs of my knuckles, and I needed to tell myself she hadn't destroyed herself to save me.

She was so wet I got three fingers deep inside her with no resistance, and she exposed her throat again.

"Are you sure?" I asked again.

"Yes." She groaned, reaching for the headboard.

"Hush now. Don't move or talk."

Slowly circling her clit, then moving back and forth. Sliding into her pussy, twitching my finger on her G-spot. I controlled her with one hand. I didn't need pain or bonds. I only needed her arousal to make her mine.

"You love me," I said.

"Yes."

"Nothing anyone says will make me think otherwise." With two quick strokes, her back arched. "Not Ronin. Not even you." I slid my fingers inside her, leaving her clit unfulfilled and rewarming her pussy.

She was hovering on the edge, and with every move, I halved the distance between her and her orgasm.

"When did you know it was the shots?"

"After you were stop-lossed. Then I saw the videos of you in the room. Saw your files. Ronin said... oh God. You should stop if you want me to talk."

"Breathe, baby. Just breathe. Tell me what he said."

Her chest heaved. "If they could cure PTSD, they could make better doctors and soldiers, but you had a childhood with... you didn't tell the whole story. And it was... so hard. The serum opened doors, and you split to... handle... the... detachment..."

"It was happening before I went to Blackthorne."

Her voice came back in soft groans. "Fallujah. It was the synthetic amphetamine in Fallu..."

Her vowel trailed off as I rubbed her hard and fast enough to give her an orgasm that sent her body into convulsions. All four fingers flat on her cunt, I leaned over her as her mouth opened wide in a soundless cry and tears streamed down the side of her face.

"You did it to me," I growled, moving my hand even after the orgasm turned painful.

"I did. Oh, God. I did."

"What should I do with you?"

"I'm sorry. Please. Please."

She didn't ask me to stop, so I kept working on her, holding her down as she writhed.

"You broke me, baby. Come again. Give me another one...right now."

She came onto my hand, letting loose a scream that was neither pleasure nor pain but an overload of both.

Jerking against me, clutching the sheets, she wept, but she did not ask me to stop.

I slowed down, then stopped, cupping her in my hand. I stretched my body parallel to hers. She was past words, breasts rising and falling quickly, eyes wide, expression drained. Exactly where I wanted her.

"What did you know?"

"I suspected something was off with the synthetic. But not this. I didn't suspect it would tear you apart."

Her expression pleaded with me to understand, but I already understood more than I wanted to.

"Why was it suspicious?"

"The indications sheet was keyed to the intake form. If you answered yes to certain questions, you couldn't get it, but I didn't think about *why* those questions. I trusted it."

"Trust is a mistake." I leaned into her until I could smell the regret on her skin. "Precision is the only thing that matters."

"It's my fault," she whispered with her eyes closed against my stare. "I know."

It wasn't her fault. I shouldn't have even let the thought cross my mind. She'd been as much of a pawn as I'd been.

"I told you that you loved me," I said. "Did I lie?"

She turned from the middle distance, steadily meeting my gaze for the first time since I'd come in. "No."

"I lied." I sat up straight with my hand flat between her breasts, feeling her heart beat against my palm. "Precision isn't the only thing that matters. Love matters too. You broke me, but you loved me whole again. What am I supposed to do?"

"Love me back."

It was the first demand she'd made of me since I walked in. Her voice had become steady and certain.

"I do," I said. "Before you, I was sure of everything. I had it all worked out. Now, because of you, I don't know anything. I'm lost in my own life, and I love you for it."

She reached up to my neck and pulled me over her. I kissed her. The taste of regret was gone.

"Be sure of me," she said, shifting her body under mine.

"You're the one indisputable thing in my life." I wedged my hips between her legs. "The only thing I live for. It's you, baby. You're gravity. You're the sky. You're the air. You're the first breath in the morning and my dreams at night. I'm sure of you because you're mine."

She put her hand on my cheek and smiled. I entered her. She was soft and wet, yielding and demanding. I bit her shoulder when she asked, sucking her skin raw. She scratched my back when she climaxed and thrust hard against me when I came.

I was still inside her, kissing the red patch on her shoulder, when she fell asleep. I shifted my weight off her chest, stroking her cheeks and neck, until I fell asleep too.

———

IT WAS STILL DARK when I turned on the shower. The showerhead was built into the wall above a drain in the floor, making the entire room into a shower stall. A makeshift curtain cut the room in half. I could have made it back to base and put my clean body into clean clothes, but her water was hotter and I didn't have to share the bathroom with two dozen other guys.

The door opened, and the curtain snapped aside.

"Hey," Greyson said. I only noticed her eyes stayed on mine when I stopped staring at her body.

"It's three in the morning," I said. "You have time to sleep."

She walked past the curtain and got under the water. "I have a lot to do." The streams fell over her hair, turning it from medium brown to sable. "And I can't just sit here and wait around for hours."

Magnificent. I ran my hands down the fall of her hair and to her lower back. She snatched the washcloth off the ring and soaped it.

"I want to see you tonight." I cupped her ass.

"Sure." She worked the cloth over her body with disappointing efficiency.

"Why are you in such a hurry?"

"Antsy. That's all."

Catching a line of lather making its way down her back, I stroked her, letting my erection press gently against her bottom.

"Ten minutes." I kissed her shoulder.

She stepped under the water and let the soap run off her, turning to face me with her head back. Her exposed throat made my balls ache.

Running the back of my hand over her nipple, I said,

"Maybe twenty." I grabbed shampoo with my free hand. "Half an hour tops."

She straightened her neck, looking at me with my boner and shampoo in my hand, a cascade of water dripping down her chin. "Can't. I'm skipping hair."

She got on her tiptoes to kiss me, then went past the curtain to dry off quickly and economically, as if she had somewhere to go.

Chapter Four

GREYSON

Caden was in the shower when I woke. I'd opened my eyes, compelled to do something, but I didn't know what. Everything. Up and out of bed. In the shower. Out the door before the sunrise. It was a work day in the Green Zone.

I blew through reports, writing up the final destination of Caden's vial without excuses or reasons. Just the facts, ma'am.

"Grey." Ronin appeared in my doorway before anyone else arrived in the office.

"Yeah."

"I want to ask—"

"Coffee," I said, standing. "Ask while we're walking."

I brushed past him, and he rushed to keep up. "The BiCam—"

I was already on the next idea. "If you have to fire me,"—I took the stairs two at a time—"then fire me. Don't waste my time. But I'm not quitting."

"I need to know—"

I slapped open the door to the cafeteria, leaving him behind.

HOW HAD ONLY two hours passed since I'd woken up? Only a few seconds to cross the cafeteria to the already-burned coffee the night staff had set up by the empty steam table? It seemed as if time used to be a flat sheet of paper that was now folded into an origami box.

I looped two mug handles in one finger and dropped them on the stainless countertop.

"We need to do a workup on you," Ronin said.

"I'm fine." I poured coffee into each cup. "The effects are less and less. I felt the jolt and crash from the B12."

And the splitting sky—

You were tired.

—as if the bowl over the earth had cracked—

You were stressed.

—into two blue eyes watching me—

You were worried about Caden.

—and I was going to slip into the dark fissure between them.

Quit it. You're sane. You have this.

"I believe you," he said casually, dropping creamer into his cup. "But we need data."

"Of course. Speaking of data, I need to go to the hospital and check on two subjects before they're shipped out."

"Then let's get started."

—————

I WAS JUMPING out of my skin, but I'd answered the questions on the form fully, using complete, cogent sentences. Some repeated the same query with different words so that inconsistencies could be noted. I wasn't born yesterday.

The black-walled room was identical to the one in New York. It even smelled like the gilded grime of Manhattan.

"You ready?" Ronin's voice came over the speakers.

"Yes." What I meant was "Get on with it."

With a click, the *soo-hoo* recording started. The anonymous woman's soothing voice seemed drunk to me, like a 45 rpm record played on 33, but I closed my eyes and stayed with it. No reason not to do it right.

I started to feel light-headed. Floaty. The pressure of the chair under me lessened. The flyaway hair on the top of my head bent as if it were touching the ceiling, which I knew was impossible. I was just—

Upward
Crunching overhead
Eyes shut, I saw everything
And nothing
Above and below
Blue, so blue
The sky above crunching

Paper-thin layers of glass cracking
The pressure on my head was enormous
Flakes of sapphire falling on my cheeks
Pushing through the bowl over the earth
Scratching my face
Gravity in reverse
Falling up
Shattering the sky
Into infinite, starless space
And falling so far, so fast
The pool below, glowing turquoise in the underwater
lights
A sky-blue rectangle in darkness
It raced toward me
Cool condensation on my face
I hovered an inch above it, flailing
A moment of conviction
I did the right thing
Before I dropped like a stone

THE END of the fall was the surface below. I expected pain. Consequences. Death.

Instead, there was relief. Release. Like bonds untied so aching shoulders could move and a sense that where submission ended, responsibility began.

But responsibility to what? To whom?

Thankfully, I got a call to the hospital. I couldn't be in that office another second. I had to *go.*

Once outside, I stood stock-still right outside the Blackthorne offices, in a sand-floored parking lot.

What had been Caden's cure? Trapped in complete darkness with a woman he loved. A pregnancy. The smell of blood and a feeling of responsibility.

I saw more differences than similarities between what had happened in the basement and what had happened under the rubble, but they had been enough. Not that it mattered in my case. I didn't have a childhood trauma. I'd been loved and nurtured by my parents, then my friends, then my husband.

I didn't have a moment to recreate.

What if I didn't have a cure?

What if the thing that had broken Caden was the only thing that could have cured him?

What if the fact that I wasn't broken meant I couldn't be fixed?

I backed up to the wall, trying to breathe slowly and deeply. After the bioenergetics session, the split was louder, more demanding. I couldn't ignore this. I couldn't pretend it would go away.

What is your fear?

Call it by its name.

Heights. Losing Caden. Cancer. Death.

Imagine the fear as an object.

Which one? They were normal. All standard. None stuck out as something that needed to be dealt with.

Give your fear a shape and a color.

Put it in a place and leave it there. Observe it. Note its dimensions and its depth. Describe its boundaries.

This wasn't working. My fears had no boundaries.

Fears with shape and weight were the demons of a sound mind.

God help me.

RESPITE WAS A WORD.

The word had a force, and it pushed against my consciousness like a bulldozer on a building. I heard it in the silence and in the whisper of the desert wind. The hum of the computer fan and the edge of Dana's words as she came to tell me to go out to the landing pad to see off two of our subjects. I was late, and I had to sign them off.

They looked great. They were great. Mentally, all great. But the whispers with counterarguments were everywhere.

Not great.

This was what Caden had gone through. I knew it. Belief that I could handle it was a habit. Running through lists of reasonable explanations was a professional routine. I still assumed I was tired or hungry but in control of my mind. If I could think about something else, it would go away.

But I couldn't run fast enough to the landing pad. Couldn't find distractions deep enough in the feel of the air on my face or the fingernail I dug into my palm.

Respite.

If I could just taste the thought, I'd know what it was. I could accept or reject. In the rattling of the earth as I went to the waiting chopper, I let it touch the tip of my tongue, accepting its push on my consciousness.

It tasted like poison.

"Thank you for holding them!" I shouted over the beating chopper blades, my hair whipping out of its ponytail strand by strand as the chopper took off with Blackthorne's two subjects.

Colonel DeLeon gave me a thumbs-up and jogged off the pad. I followed, glad to be moving.

"Did you get what you needed?" she asked when it was quiet enough to talk.

"Yes. Sorry it took so long. I got held up at the office."

The *soo-hoo*ing had seemed to go on forever, but not as long as it had taken me to write down what I'd felt and seen during the circular breathing exercise.

"They looked better," she said. "Whatever you're doing, it's good work."

"Thank you."

Her hand was on the door to the hospital. I wanted to go forward, but she was stopping me, and this created a nagging irritation.

"Your last name's Frazier?" Another nagging irritation. Easy rhetorical questions.

"Yes. Why?"

"California? Your family's from San Diego?"

I assumed Caden had told her, but the question was ill-timed, and I had to bite back a snotty retort for Caden's sake. "Officially."

"Follow me, please."

She strode through the halls as though she owned the joint, chin up, looking ahead in such a way as to say,

"Don't stop me with anything less than a life-and-death emergency." Opening a nondescript door, she ushered me through and closed it behind us.

The desks were wide shelves mounted to the wall. Three computers and a line of binders. Two beat-up office chairs. She held her hand over one, and I sat in it, then she leaned over a keyboard.

"I hope I'm wrong," she said as she tapped. "But it's not a secret, and I don't know if your employer's looping you in."

She got out of the way of the screen. It was split into six boxes, each with a photo of a soldier. All men. Four white. Two African American. One I recognized.

Jacob Frazier.

"What—?"

"His squad was ambushed outside Al Taqa. These six were captured."

Captured.

Jake's been captured.

I said it to myself over and over, looking at his deadpan expression on the computer screen.

"Is he related?" she asked.

"He's my big brother."

And I owe him everything.

I didn't know where the debt came from. It was more of a feeling than a narrative.

"They're searching for them," she said. "I'd rather you found out from me than some rumor in the cafeteria."

What were they doing to him? How much pain was he in? How much panic?

Jake was tough, but torture broke the strongest of us.

It bent the mind around the body. I'd seen it in my patients. Resilient men and women were broken by the force of it.

"Wifey," DeLeon said tenderly, "they're going to find them."

"Where are they?" My question made no sense in light of the fact that the army was looking, but I was only thinking in straight lines. "They have to know. They can't *not know*."

"They—"

"No! I don't want to hear it. I want details."

She leaned on the counter, crossing her arms and watching me as my blood raced and my face got hot. Behind her, my brother's face and five others looked flatly through a screen. Lies of time.

"I might know someone who can fill in some blanks."

"I want to meet them. Now."

"Tonight. Maybe. Royal Rose is a big spook hangout."

"Spook" meant CIA, and the Royal Rose was a bar on the other side of the Green Zone.

Fine. I'd go to the spook bar and grill the CIA. I had plans with Caden. I loved him, but I didn't want to go *back* to my apartment to fall *back* into his arms. I wanted to find out what had happened to my brother. Forward to him because he needed me.

I stood, calmer with the prospect of doing something. "What time?"

Chapter Five

CADEN

Maybe I wasn't the most perceptive guy who ever walked the earth. Maybe I was a little detached and self-involved. When it came to other people, I could be slow. I processed vital data about patients and casualties quickly, but data about their moods and thoughts? I had no idea how to analyze that, and I didn't care to.

At the morning staff meeting, we were warned a dozen diplomats were landing at Baghdad International. They'd take Airport Road twelve kilometers to the Green Zone. We were all on call because that was the only stretch of road between the airport and the Green Zone, and it wasn't called IED Alley for nothing.

A couple of choppers dropped down like clockwork, and the meeting ended as we all ran to the landing pad.

"Wasn't bad," said the kid with a bullet bite in his calf. "We got 'em through."

"What's the trick?" I asked just to keep him talking while I examined the wound.

"Keep pushing. Just keep pushing."

I WAS CLEANING fragments out of someone's flexor carpi when I decided not to say, "He'll be home getting his wife off in no time." One, it was inappropriate, and I had functioning social filters.

But there was a second reason I didn't say that or anything, and I put it together during the busy work of cleaning shrapnel out of a wrist and arm.

I couldn't stop thinking about Greyson.

How she'd changed.

When I'd arrived the night before, she'd been lethargic, but more precisely? She'd been emotionally listless as well. She hadn't asked questions or answered sharply. She hadn't pushed back on my manipulation.

It wasn't the first time she'd been sick, but it was the first time she'd been mentally weak.

And in the morning?

Fully in motion but without the cutting sensitivity I took for granted.

She'd said she was feeling the effects but she was fine. Had she split?

My Damon self had battled for expression when the sun set, but she'd been changed during the night.

If she'd changed. Big *if*. But if she'd changed, it wasn't with the appearance of the sun. It was something else. I stitched up the hand, putting together every word she'd said and how she'd said it.

Be sure of me.

Last words I remembered her saying before good night and the soft breaths of sleep.

Be sure of me.

A command or a request?

"I have to apologize in advance," DeLeon said in the scrub room.

"I don't give advance pardons."

"Wif—" She caught herself mid-nickname. "Your wife's brother's been captured."

"Jake?"

"Yes."

Jake had been her protector and mentor. She loved him with a fierceness she usually reserved for me.

"Are you sure?"

"She confirmed."

"Fuck. How is she?"

"Motivated. I'm taking her to the Royal Rose tonight to pry one of my contacts for details."

I didn't know whether to thank her or stop her. Greyson already wasn't herself. How was she going to react? How was she reacting right now? Would the news make the split I suspected even worse?

"Cancel it," I said. "Say something came up. Go without her. But cancel. Please."

"Only for you, blue eyes." She started to walk away, then spoke over her shoulder. "Only for you."

I was upset about Jake. He was a good man, but my wife wasn't going to have such a blithe reaction.

I SHOULD HAVE TOLD Ronin about my suspicions about her split, but I wasn't in the mood for him. I didn't want to commiserate or brainstorm with him about the state of my wife's mind, especially with Jake in Iraqi hands.

Finding her was like hitting a moving target. Someone said she was in the supply room, then the chow hall, then the parking lot, then the landing pad. Once I got off work, I continued the chase to the Blackthorne office, where she was on her way out of a tiny refrigerated room.

"What are you doing here?"

I held the door open before it could close behind her. "I want to talk to you."

I nudged her back into the room. She didn't budge. Not an inch. She pursed her mouth tightly and tried to stare me down. What game was she playing?

"I said I wanted to talk to you."

"If I wanted to go backward, I'd have moved already."

The longer the staring contest went on, the more convinced I was that I was looking at half a woman. Greyson in her full splendor would never have looked away, but she never fought me over small things. She never grasped at winning for the sake of it. She would have explained why she couldn't go back, made plans to meet elsewhere, all while staring me down. No woman's submission had ever been more voluntary than hers.

But this woman?

She was egging me on for the sake of it. It was either back down or be baited, and I would not be baited.

Nor would I back down.

"I heard about Jake."

"There's not much I can do, is there?"

"I know you. You never do nothing." I stood immobile and locked hard on her face.

"My office," she said.

I broke the stare, stepping backward so she could lead me.

***

"I'M sure they're going to find him," I said when she closed the door, cutting off the sound of keyboards and ringing phones, leaving only the traffic and wind from the open window.

"You don't look sure. You look hopeful. Not sure."

"Fine." I threw myself onto the couch. "Hopeful. He welcomed me into the family on day one, and he was always good to you."

She didn't sit next to me. She leaned on her desk with her arms crossed. "You're talking about him in the past tense."

"Are you all right? Are you upset?"

"Of course I'm upset. What do you think? Who knows what they're doing to him? I don't know if he's even alive or if he wishes he was dead." She covered her face with her hands as if she wanted to mask her emotions with her hands. "And I can't do anything. I'm a few miles away, and I can't do anything."

"You're going to meet an intelligence guy tonight apparently?"

She dropped her hands. "I just want information. I have to know as much as they'll tell me."

"What are you going to do with that information besides make yourself crazy?"

Her lips tightened to the length of a matchstick. She bowed her head quickly, turning away so she could face the open window. She hooked her finger in the grate.

"If you're at the right angle, you can see the Tigris River from here." She pressed her cheek to the grate to find the angle. "Sometimes I watch the Humvees and trucks going out to the port and see the boats and I wonder what it's like to go someplace. To just run into the unknown. It's like I'm stuck in a matrix of limited possibilities. Going around in a circle, like that carnival ride where you stand against the walls of a round room and it spins and spins. Then the floor drops out, and you don't fall, but you're stuck to that wall by centrifugal force, just spinning and spinning." She turned to me fully, leaving her thumb and pinkie hooked in the grate. "What does it take to get out of it?"

"The walls drop, and you go flying."

She sat in the chair perpendicular to the couch, knees apart, leaning forward with a keen attention to what she said and what she meant. "My brother is outside that spinning room."

"You're not talking about *going*. You're talking about *being thrown*. You're talking about being powerless."

"I don't think I can find out how far I can go on my own. I don't think any of us can."

"Greyson." I sat up.

"Listen, think about it."

"What, exactly, are you talking about?"

"We can't push against our own limits because they're *our limits*. It's like a pot can't ever get any hotter than the flame under it."

"I mean, what are you trying to do? You want to get out of some loop, but you can't do it yourself, and hell knows I'm not on board for this. Who's pushing? *What's* pushing?" My hands were clawed as if I wanted to strangle her. My muscles were coiled tight.

She saw my frustration, and it did not interest her. "Don't worry about it."

"Greyson..."

"I'm just thinking out loud." She dropped her hand and stood behind her desk, shuffling papers from one side to the other. She stopped at a small slip of paper I couldn't see from my angle. She slid it away from the stack and continued moving the papers around.

"Did you split?" I asked.

She froze with a page in each hand, six inches over the desk, hovering.

"After the shot, did you split like I did? Is there a part of you trapped in darkness?"

"No." She put both pages in a single pile. "I just want to know where my brother is."

Her intercom buzzed, and Dana's voice came over it. "Dr. Frazier? Your appointment is here."

"Please excuse me," she said. "I have work to do."

I stood. She put her hand on my arm to guide me out, but I didn't move.

"You're not going tonight," I said. "I'll see you later."

I THOUGHT my respect for my wife immense. I'd assumed I was maxed out on admiration. But when I realized what was happening, that respect unfolded again and again, taking up more space in my heart than I'd thought I had.

In New York, she'd faced an impossible situation. A new city with few friends. A husband acting in strange and dangerous ways. She'd stayed strong and competent where I would have fallen apart.

At least, I assumed I would have. Faced with her need, maybe I had the strength. I wouldn't abandon her.

Maybe I was the one unfolding.

Ronin had to meet me at the hospital. A medevac landed before he got there. He waited for me to get out of surgery. I chalked that up to him either giving a shit about Greyson or being worried about his job.

"So?" He stood when I met him in the administration waiting room.

"I don't have a lot of time."

"Fine. How is she?"

"Passive one minute, aggressive the next."

"Are you sure it's not mood swings?"

That comment didn't deserve a response.

"We've got to get her in for more sessions," he said. "The last one was inconclusive."

He was worried, insomuch as he ever showed me anything but distant professionalism. The slight concern I detected rang like an alarm.

"She thinks she's fine," I said.

"Does she?"

"Her brother was captured. She's not fine."

"I was wondering if I should tell her."

"You don't have to. I can't tell if she's acting strangely because of the shot or what, but I want you to keep an eye on her."

"That I can do."

DELEON CANCELLED THEIR DATE. I half expected my wife to find a way to run across the Green Zone by herself so she could ask random intelligence officers about Jake, but she answered the door to her little studio with the phone wedged between her shoulder and ear.

"Okay, I understand," she said into the phone. "I love you too." She hung up.

"Who was that?"

"My mother."

"How is she?"

"We agreed on twenty-two hundred," she said, closing the door behind me. "You're late."

I looked her up and down. Her hair was brushed and clean. She wore sweatpants low on her waist and a tight, dull-green tee that ended just above her navel, casually exposing the soft curve of her hips and stomach. Her feet were bare on the cheap Persian rug.

"Nice to see you too."

Her hand was still on the knob, as if she wanted to open it and run out. I flipped the deadbolt.

"Were you the one to tell your parents?" I asked.

"They knew. Dad blew it off. Says Jake's going to be fine. Worrying won't help."

"And?"

"And he's right. I know he's right. But I still feel trapped in a spinning room."

There were a few ways to ground her. One came to mind quickly.

"Take your clothes off," I commanded.

She walked to the other side of the room. Not walked. She *stalked* there as if she was agitated and there was a purpose to the relocation.

This was new. All of it was new. I had no idea what she wanted, much less needed. Did she need to release her energies? Go for a run through Baghdad? Did she need to be soothed? Controlled?

I sensed the adrenaline running through her veins. I wanted to take her pulse, but I already knew her blood was pounding.

"We should go to Royal Rose," she said.

"It's past curfew. Go tomorrow."

If she wasn't Greyson, I would have thought she was avoiding me. But she was who she was, and I was her mate. She wanted to leave, and it wasn't because of me.

That confidence bore another conclusion.

Whatever I did was what she needed.

"Remember a second ago?" I said. "When I told you to take your clothes off?"

"I can't... I have to keep going."

"Where?"

"Anywhere. Something isn't finished, and it's not getting finished here."

When she finally met my eyes, I saw dark circles under confusion and aggression. She'd gotten up before three in the morning, and unlike me, she was a sleeper. Ten hours if she had her way.

I stood in front of her. She looked at me, then over my shoulder.

"You keep looking at the door like someone's going to walk through it."

She looked up at me. All the confusion and aggression were there, along with something else. A plea for help.

"You don't need to go out. You need to get some sleep."

And, with that, maybe the change. I needed to see if she'd wake a different woman.

Again, I was struck with my ignorance of how to help her and my trust that whatever I did was what she needed. I couldn't imagine one without the other. My ignorance without confidence would break me. Confidence without knowledge of my ignorance would break her.

"I can't sleep," she said. "I tried."

"Do you want to speak frankly?" I said. "Or do you want me to take what's mine?"

"Are those my only choices?"

"Following you all over Baghdad isn't on the list."

"Don't follow then."

She tried to push past me, but I wrapped my arm

around her, pulling her close so I could growl in her ear. "I'd rather you tell me what's going on."

"Noted."

"If you insist."

I threw her on the bed. She landed on her back, and I expected her to leap up and punch me in the face. Instead, she got up on her elbows.

"Are you going to take your clothes off, or am I going to do it?"

"Is this how it's going to be?" The question was so pointed it had a vector all its own.

"You tell me." I leaned over her, knees on the bed, knuckles digging divots into the mattress. "Are you going to be honest with me?"

"Fuck you! I am being honest. I've never lied to you."

"Then are you going to be honest with yourself? Because I'm not as patient as you. I'm not half as nice. You're going to talk to me, or I'm going to take what's mine."

"What if I tell you to stop?"

"Then it's not mine, is it?"

A shade of her aggression wore away, and a few layers of confusion turned into attention.

"Are you talking?" I asked. "Or am I taking?"

She laid her hands on my chest. She was going to push me off her, which meant she either needed space for talking or she was telling me to stop.

"I'm not in the mood to talk," she said. "Take what's yours. But I'm not stripping for you just because you say so."

"Then I'll fuck you with your clothes on." I pulled her

shirt over her bare breasts. "I really don't give a shit." I tweaked a nipple and sucked it between my teeth. She jerked her hips and groaned. "Are these tits mine?"

She groaned again.

"Answer me." I twisted the other one and resumed sucking. It got hard and long in my mouth.

"The tits are yours."

"Good girl."

I kneeled over her as I undid my pants and pulled out my erection. When she looked at it the way she always did, like a lioness terrified of her prey but too hungry not to pounce, it throbbed harder. I swiped the drop of clear liquid off the tip with two fingers and placed them on her bottom lip.

"Is this mouth mine?"

She nodded, and I shoved them in her mouth.

"Suck."

She closed her lips over them and pulled. The sensation went right to my balls.

"That's good. Very good. Open wide. All the way down." She opened her throat, and I owned it, taking her breath away and giving it back.

I took my hand away from her and wiped the spit onto my dick, fisting it for her as she watched with her shirt pulled over her hard-kissed tits. She started to get her hands at her waistband, but I grabbed her wrists and held them over her head firmly, but without aggravating her injury. With her arms up, her breasts went higher, tighter.

"Too late." I put my free hand over the silver line left of her sternum. "Whose scar is this?"

"Yours."

Drawing my hand down her belly, I asked, "Whose is this?"

"Yours."

After untying her waistband, I grabbed a fistful of her sweatpants and yanked them down to just below the triangle between her legs.

"Caden," she gasped. "My cunt is yours."

"I knew you'd come around." I got my fingers in her folds, and she writhed with pleasure while I held down her arms. "And this?" With my wet fingers, I circled her asshole.

"Take it. If you want it. Take it."

Letting her wrists go, I pulled her knees up to her chest and her waistband down to midthigh, exposing her clit, her cunt, her ass. Everything. I rubbed from one end of her seam to the other, savoring the ridges and bumps, the caress of one entrance and the tension of the other. I left no nerve unstimulated, inside or out, until she broke out in a sweat, grinding her hips into me.

"Yes."

"You're obsessed with finishing something. But I'm the one who's going to finish you tonight."

I toyed with her until her body was slick with sweat and every touch made her shudder. Then slowly, so slowly, with the sweatpants stretched between her thighs, I slid my dick inside her.

"All the way," she whispered, hungry, begging.

"I'll take what's mine. Any. Way. I. Want."

With the last four words, I pulled out and in just

enough to be felt. Just enough to drive her crazy. Then I buried myself so deep she howled.

Her legs over my shoulders, the pants against my chest, my own waistband restricting me, I took her hard.

I knew my wife. I knew how to fuck her. I knew what she liked and how she got off.

But no matter how hard I drove, she didn't come.

No matter how deep I went, she stayed on the edge.

I bit her breast, pinched her hips, gave her as much pain as I dared, and still, she cried and scratched but didn't come.

"Fuck," I said, coming inside her.

I kissed her neck and down her belly when her fingers tightened in my hair.

"Stop," she said. I looked up at her, and she stared down at me. "I need to drive this."

"Excuse me?"

She sat up and pulled off her pants. "I can't be a passenger right now." She peeled her shirt off as I got up and stood by the side of the bed with my dick out.

"I'm not done with you," I said.

"I know." Naked, she swung her legs over the edge of the bed, sitting straight. She yanked my pants down. "Foot."

I raised one foot, then the other so she could get my pants off.

"You might need to give me five minutes," I said at half-mast.

"I don't think so."

Taking my ass in her hands, she pulled my hips

toward her and licked me clean from the underside of my balls to the tip of my dick.

"When we met," I said, taking my shirt off as she worked on me, "I had no idea you'd be this filthy."

"Would you have married me?"

"I was a nice guy back then." The touch of her tongue went from ticklish to something deeper. "You corrupted me."

She ran her tongue over my hardening length. "The gentleman doth protest too much."

I laughed, running my fingers through her hair, fully hard in under five minutes.

"You wanted to drive?" I asked.

"Yeah."

There wasn't enough furniture in this apartment. Or at least not the *right* furniture. I helped Greyson up and led her to the cheap loveseat. I sat on the edge and pulled her close until her knees were on either side of me, and I leaned back as I let my hands roam her body, finding the crook between her legs.

She stayed my hand. "Don't."

She put my palms on her hips, lowered herself onto me. I watched my cock disappear inside her. When I moved my hands to her breasts, she moved them to her hips again.

"You're getting bossy."

"No backseat driving."

I let her set the pace. Let her push against me. Let her move any way she liked. She was unbelievably sexy when she was in charge.

"Fuck," she grunted, leaning over me. "I can't."

"I have all night, baby."

"I need... something."

"I can hurt you a hundred ways. Just say the word."

She thought about it, then sat straight again. "Something else." She took my right hand and laid it between her breasts. "I'm spinning." She put my hand on her throat, pressing my thumb and middle finger to opposite sides. "I need a straight line out. Give it to me."

Her veins pulsed under my hand, and the lump in her throat shifted when she swallowed. The control she offered was so precious that I took a moment before agreeing to it.

"Come on me." I tightened my hand just a little. "Use me to fuck yourself."

Her eyes on me, her jaw in the cradle of my hand, she moved again, and I drove a little, moving with her. All my focus was on her reaction, her pleasure, the release of tension from her face.

When her lips opened and her eyelids fluttered, she was back on the edge. I tightened my hand. "Say no while you still can."

"Yes."

She groaned under my hand. The orgasm was pushing at the boundaries, looking for a way in.

Tighter.

She went rigid mid-orgasm, shaking uncontrollably. I wrapped my other arm around her to bring her into me, pushing her clit against my body as the last of her air gave out. Her pussy squeezed, pulsing around my shaft, but I couldn't come. I couldn't lose control while I had her life in my hands.

When I was sure she'd peaked, I let go, and she pulled in air like a drowning woman, then let out a long vowel sound that told me her body had elongated the orgasm while it dealt with the lack of air and exploded when she breathed again.

She collapsed on me.

"Hey," I said, pulling her hair away from her face. "Let me look at you."

She groaned, getting her arms under her with her head still bowed.

I reached past the curtain of hair for her chin. "Hey. Come on. Look at me. I need to see if you're all right."

I wanted to check her body, but when she looked at me, it wasn't her body that needed my attention.

"Greyson?"

She just looked at me, and I wondered what her name was.

Chapter Six

GREYSON

Distant in the darkness, a blue dot appeared, coming faster and faster, revealing its shape.

Speeding toward me, the blue rectangle glowed and shimmered. Under the water, black lines divided lanes.

Diving pools didn't have lanes, but the one hurtling toward me did.

Black hashes joined the lines, defining themselves into letters, numbers, instructions. The edges of the rectangle curled, and when I hit the surface at an impossible speed, the water was as dry as paper, and I was plunged into darkness so Respite could remember.

SAN DIEGO
JULY - 1992

I TRIED to keep my printing tight and clear, but I didn't feel well. My stomach felt like a dirty washcloth, wrung out and stuffed too high up my rib cage, regurgitating bitter yuck into my dry mouth that toothpaste couldn't cover. My head had a rock embedded on the left side where my brain should have been.

I saw through a layer of gunk as I tried to copy my driver's license number onto the blue form. I shook the pen. Copied the first three characters. Blinked gunk away.

Was that a 5 or an S?

"Do you have an idea when you'd like to start?" The recruiter folded her hands over the stack of papers I'd brought. She was white with a gash of red lipstick at the bottom of her face and flat platinum hair tied into a bun. It had the faintest line of brown at the roots.

My purple nail polish was chipped, and I had to tilt my head just so to see her through the fall of hair over my face. I'd dyed it Nuclear Black in the bathroom sink. I liked the idea of a black so black it could wipe out a city. "I get to pick?"

"You test now but... might want to go to college first?"

I went back to the forms. "I'm done." The pen made a colorless M-shaped furrow in the paper.

"Get married?"

"Not happening." I shook the pen and made circles in the corner of the page until the ink ran.

"Those are just examples."

"I can start right away."

She cleared her throat. "Do you have any idea what you want to do? As a job?"

"Whatever." I stopped writing. Tapped the pen. Put

my nail between my teeth and removed it quickly. I wasn't supposed to bite my nails. I looked at her to see if she'd noticed, then I realized my answer wasn't going to fly. "I don't..." *Tap-tap.* "I don't want to hurt anyone. I want to serve. Not kill."

"There are plenty of ways to try to avoid that, but in the end, you'll have to serve in the capacity you're required."

"I can live with that."

"You're probably going to want to cut your hair before you test."

I flicked my head to get the fall of hair off my eye. "Sure."

"And if you come in without makeup, that's fine. Just get it all off."

She touched the outer corner of her eye, and I mirrored her. A streak of sludge was left on my fingertip.

"Yeah." I snapped a tissue from the box on her desk. "Okay."

"Greyson?" Her voice was kind but firm as she tapped my hand. "Don't worry. We're going to turn you into a soldier."

I believed her, and in that belief, I found comfort.

FEAR DIDN'T KEEP me still, nor did an inability to leave. I didn't want to move. I wanted to watch my story play over and over. The phones ringing at the recruitment office. The way the recruiter's lipstick ended in a crisp line across a bump that crested the boundary of her lip. The tang of alcohol seeping through my skin. I could remember every detail as if I was living it—except the reason I was there.

When I got up to go to the bathroom, it was with a certain resentment of my bodily functions. Caden was gone; I didn't know for how long. I was supposed to go to work but wouldn't.

A part of me was crying to get the fuck up, get the fuck out, move it like it mattered, but that part of me wasn't in charge.

The part of me on an infinite loop of past details was in complete control, and I had no choice but to watch as the story unspooled backward.

JAKE PULLED into the strip mall recruiting office and put the car into park. It was hot as hell, and it wasn't even noon.

"You go quicker if you have everything." His eyes were red-rimmed, and he smelled of sanitary wipes. "Passport. Driver's license."

"I have them." I pulled my knapsack out from between my knees.

"All your transcripts?"

"Back to third grade."

"Did you find the immunization records?"

"Jakey, I have everything."

He looked in the rearview. I didn't know what for. Maybe he was checking his own face to see if he'd aged in the past six hours. He had. "All right. I'll go talk to Mom and Dad."

"You don't have to."

"I know."

I pulled the latch on the car door. The dashboard beeped. This was it. The moment my life split into the dozens of things I could have done and the one thing I did.

"Thank you," I said without looking at him. I was looking into my lap, where I could see my raggedy nails half-covered in chipped purple polish. I'd wanted to clean them up but had run out of time.

No. It hadn't been time.

I'd run out of desire to do anything to make this easier on myself.

"I love you, sis." Jake laid his hand on the back of my neck and gave me a little shake.

"I love you too."

"You're going to be fine."

"Don't make me cry, fuckhead."

He put both hands on the wheel. "Then get out of here."

I flipped the fall of hair out of my eyes and got out, dragging my knapsack. I closed the door, took three steps to the double glass doors, and...

"GREY, BABY."

His voice overlaid the hundredth time I walked the strip mall pavement from the car to the recruiting office, skirting a beige wad of gum shaped like a rabbit.

Grey baby grey baby grey baby.

My face tickled when he pulled hair away from it. The screen telling the story flickered, and the details got muddy. They needed my attention. They needed to be memorized and cataloged. But with the flicker of that screen, desire came through. A desire to do things. To move. To lurch forward with big steps toward a goal.

The flicker straightened itself again, and I read every sign, decal, and flyer on the glass doors as if time had slowed down and I'd stopped myself from going in.

"How long has she been like this?"

That was Ronin.

"Twenty-three hundred."

"What was happening right before?"

Before.

His hands were on my throat, and I was having the longest orgasm of my life. Would he tell Ronin that? Because then he'd know, and I'd know, and everyone would know how to stop the story so I could move and breathe again.

"She slept for a moment."

Had I? I'd felt awake. Maybe he thought I'd gone black. I could have corrected him. We could have talked about it. But I didn't want to. Or more accurately, I didn't want to want to.

Caden: "I'm taking her to the hospital."

Ronin: "Let us take her. We know what we're dealing

with."

Caden: "No, you don't. I'm not interested in protecting you or the people you work for. I'm interested in protecting my wife. Get in the way of that. Just try."

Ronin: "I'll get the car."

Footsteps and a door closing. None of it was as clear as the changing smells and sounds as I walked into the army's office in a strip mall in San Diego.

"Grey," Caden said, "I'm going to take this sheet off you and get you dressed. It's just me here."

The sheet tickled my torso as it slid down. Cool air on damp skin. His hand on my shoulder to turn me. The touch wasn't sexual, but it was a flicker in my attention. A place where two universes melted together.

I felt the desire to desire again. It pushed through and grabbed his hand.

"Grey."

I was too muddled for words, but actions were feasible. I pushed his hand to the place my legs met.

"What's happening?" he asked.

I kept the pressure on his wrist as a world opened up in the places our bodies touched. Everything was there. The screen sped up, flicked, went slow. Where we were together was where the loop ended.

"I didn't know if it was the orgasm or the lack of oxygen that changed you. I guess you're telling me."

He removed his hand. The recruiting office smelled of coffee and off-gassing. There was a tip-tapping of keyboards and the buzz of overhead lights. A deadbolt slid and clicked. The bed leaned, and Caden's voice was in my head.

"I want you to know," he said, running fingertips along my collarbone, breaking the loop, "I know what you're going through. I think I do. If it's similar." His hand circled my right breast, leaving a line of vibrating nerve endings in its wake. "I'm trying to stay calm about it because I can't help you otherwise. But I have to tell you..." He went down my belly, to the space where my thighs met. "I hate to see you like this. I hate it. I know this is as much a part of you as the woman I married, and I love every fucking piece of you. But I'm afraid we're being forced to live our lives in pieces."

With two hands, he opened my legs. I was on fire. Bloated with desire. The insides of my thighs were tender where he stroked, sensitive as new skin. My universe revolved around his touch. Everything else was bathed in a silvery gray that shimmered like a movie screen.

His hand stopped. There was a fly in the recruiting office. I heard it buzzing like a circular saw.

"I need you to say yes," he said. "I can't do this without that."

My will was tied up in my backward story, but another will needed to speak, and it would not be denied.

"Don't..."

He stopped. That wasn't what I wanted.

"—ess." I couldn't make the Y. I could only hope I was clear enough.

Caden didn't say anything. I wondered for a moment if he'd heard me, then the bed shifted with him. His hands ran the length of my body and back again, pausing to toy with my hard nipples. He opened my legs all the way, leaving me exposed, unable to resist or comply. A doll in his hands as he stroked and kissed inside my thighs before bending my knees over his shoulders.

Cool fingers slid inside me, and his thumb rubbed against my clit. I screamed for more, harder, faster, but nothing came out. I was trapped into submission by my own fugue.

"I can tell you like it," he said. "Your tits are standing on end, and you're getting wetter."

All that was true and more. The story had been mixed into the pleasure between my legs, and my will found a place to speak through. "Yes."

Fingers gone, I heard his belt. His button. A zipper. The rustle of clothing and the creak of the bed, and he bent over my folded body.

"I can't wait to hear your voice again," he whispered in my ear.

The smooth head of his cock ran along my seam, then into me, stretching me open, pushing deep against me until his body pressed my clit and jerked side to side. Warmth spread like a stain into me. My knees were pressed against my chest as he fucked me.

As the pleasure grew, so did my will. It pushed through the screen in the shape of a woman trying to run through a latex wall.

"Come on, baby," he said. "Give it to me."

The rubbery wall broke at the sharpest points. Knuckles. Knee. Nose. Yielding to the force of the oncoming climax, giving way with tiny rips that grew around the contours of my body, breaking as I came through and living inside a pleasure whose gratifications were so satisfying, so all-consuming, so temporary.

The screen was in tatters.

I was out.

CADEN SAT on the edge of the bed, rumpled but clothed.

"What do you remember?" he asked as I got dressed.

I didn't care. Remembering was the past, and I was in the future, living my next second, not my last. But where was I going? What was my future? "Nothing."

"Noth—?"

"Like I said..." I pulled my button-front shirt over my head. Easier than fastening and unfastening a bunch of—

"If you'd stop moving for a second, you might."

"I'm hungry." I jammed my heel into a shoe. "I can't think."

"It's been three days since you—"

"Let me eat first." Second shoe.

"Ronin's bringing the car. I want—"

"There's an American place a few blocks away."

I opened the door. The world. The earth. Huge. Massive. Accessible through a doorway, sucking me into the curve of infinity. I could walk straight forever and wind up exactly where I'd started... but only if I got out.

He stood. "I'll walk with—"

"You can catch up."

"Can you let me finish a sentence?"

Sure. He could finish a sentence. Outside.

THE SUN WAS a diffuse disk behind a thin veil of flying sand and heat. A convoy rolled by at half a mile a fucking hour. Five tanks and a bunch of Humvees draped in armed men. They waved. Some nodded. Two jumped off and kept us from crossing the street.

"You need to get out of the way," I said. "You're going so slow I can make it between."

"Sorry, ma'am."

I wanted to slap the mirrored sunglasses off his fucking face, but Caden had my right arm in a vise, and he growled in my ear, "Calm the fuck down."

"I *can't.*"

"Listen to me. Just pay attention to my voice. You've been in a fugue since last night. Ever since the last time I fucked you. Do you remember?"

The sex. I'd ridden him to orgasm. Could I walk down the block and go around this snail parade? No. They were standing at each intersection to prevent exactly that.

"Do you remember?" he asked again.

"I remember."

"What happened after that?"

If I wanted to think about it, I'd be thinking about it. I swung my gaze away from the troops at the corner to his eyes. The blue was not comforting. It was a reminder of everything that was broken.

"Please." I didn't know what I was pleading for.

"After that. What happened?"

I swallowed, paying attention to the way my throat opened and contracted. Sand bit my eyes. I narrowed them, bringing my husband into greater focus.

"I was enlisting. I remembered that day. It was with Jake, and I'm sure it's because he's on my mind. But it feels *bad*. I don't know how else to explain it." Bouncing, I looked up and down the block. Still trapped for the next few minutes. "It was the shot. The BiCam. Not a placebo, Caden. Not a placebo. I don't know what effect it would have had on you. Jesus, I want to strangle someone for trying to do this to you. It's awful. So awful. This isn't worth it. Nothing's worth it."

He cupped my jaw in his hands and held my eyes in place with his. "It's going to be okay."

"How?"

"I swear it, Greyson, I swear on my life I'm going to fix this. Can you believe me?"

Could I?

I believed he believed it, but the feeling of being on defense was so awkward that relief seemed impossible. The need to move-move-move to get away-away-away before I was overtaken was as mentally uncomfortable as I'd ever been.

"I feel it. It's another me. It's a me who knows things that she wants to show me. My God, Caden, she has a name. I split, and she has a fucking name. How did you cope with this?"

"I had months. This came on you quicker."

"Why?" I was suddenly desperate for some kind of answer.

"The dose maybe? Maybe years of repression made the doors open slower? I don't know." He moved his hands to my shoulders, squeezing where they met my arms. "All I know is we're going to fix it."

"When?"

"What's her name? The one you've locked away?"

"I don't want to say it."

"Say it so I know what to call her."

"Respite." I said it as if I couldn't believe it. It wasn't a name, but it was the word that came to me over and over. *Respite*. A reprieve. A suspended sentence. And the name of mental discomfort. The name of its opposite.

The convoy creaked by, and the soldier blocking us moved to the left to block two women wearing abayas that blew in the wind.

I ran across the street—toward-toward-toward.

Chapter Seven

CADEN

There were so many things I'd wanted to do. Bring her to the hospital. To Blackthorne. Home. I wanted to try circular breathing. Anything and everything...but one thing at a time.

Then she was off like a shot, across the street through a break in the line of military vehicles. She was hard to catch under the best of circumstances. When she ran, she took off as if she was taunting me to catch up.

I was in heavy boots and a uniform built for protection against harsh elements. Not speed. Not comfort. My feet were heavier than hers, and her timing had been as catlike as her risk-taking.

Guns swung toward her. Clicks echoed off the sky.

I had a choice.

Use the air in my lungs to run after her and catch her bullet-ridden body before it hit the ground. Or use that air to stop the shots.

"Hold fire!" I shouted from the deepest, widest part of my lungs.

I had no authority over these men, but I was a major and I was in uniform. I held my hands out to both hold them and show I wasn't a threat.

The convoy shut down, and men piled off the Humvees.

The guy who'd stopped us from crossing the street jogged to me. "What the fuck—?"

"She's with me!"

"Who was that?" A dusty sergeant came to the sidewalk. I looked small and sad in the mirrors of his goggles. That was intentional. Self-reflection was intimidation.

"My wife," I said, straightening so I looked a little more authoritative in the mirrors. "She's with a contracting operation."

"Is she trying to get shot?"

In his mirrored glasses, I looked at myself expectantly. Small or not, I had leaves on my collar.

"Sir," the sergeant added. "Is she trying to get shot, sir?"

"Just in a hurry, Sergeant. If you give me room, I'll be following her."

He stepped aside and kept his opinions to himself. "Let's move out!"

They hustled back to the line of trucks, and in the moments before they moved again, I dashed across.

THE GREEN ZONE was both militarized and demilitarized, with one making the other possible. The *pop-pop* of live rounds went off sixteen hours a day at the Blackthorne training compounds, where the sight of a person rappeling or jumping off the roof of a building onto a yellow-and-blue stunt bag coexisted with a Subway franchise and a makeshift Burger King.

The American place Greyson had mentioned existed in the nether region between the white-tablecloth restaurants the diplomats and businesspeople frequented and the fast-food joints the low-rent contractors went to.

I jogged after her, avoiding the piles of rubble that dotted the streets as a reminder of how we'd gotten here. When I turned the last corner, she was half a block ahead and walking into the diner. I slowed down, relieved she hadn't changed course on a whim.

"I ordered you an egg sandwich with cheese," she said when I walked in. "They only have cheddar."

Too early for lunch and too late for breakfast, the place was nearly empty. She was standing by the front counter as if she was ready to make a getaway.

I leaned over to the woman at the register. "We're having it to stay."

"Caden," Greyson said behind me, annoyed.

"Sit anywhere," the hostess said.

I took my wife gently by the elbow and guided her to the back.

"I don't want to stay," she hissed.

"Neither do I, but the convoy could be another ten minutes at the rate they were going."

She slid into the back booth facing the rest of the

room and folded her hands together on the table. I got in across from her. The window to my left was coated with a fine layer of dust.

I clasped her hands in the center of the table, squeezing briefly as if that could transmit my level of empathy. "I know what you're going through."

"Is it wrong that makes me feel less alone?"

"That's a question for a priest." I pulled our fists to my mouth, kissed her hand, and put them back on the table.

"I feel like my mind is a record that's skipping. I have this nagging pressure from 'her,' and the only thing that shuts her up is moving forward, and the space between them is just on and on."

"Where does it tell you to move forward to?"

"Just anywhere." The space between her brows knotted, and her hands tightened around mine. "And Jake. I'm so worried about him. It just says, 'Do something,' but there's nothing I can do."

"They'll find him."

"What if they don't?"

A waiter in a stained white polo shirt brought our breakfast on paper plates and left a fistful of metal silverware in the center of the table.

"Please eat."

"I'm not hungry. I mean, I'm starving actually. But this anxiety." She pressed her thumb to her sternum.

Being married to a psychiatrist had its downsides. She thought everything could be solved with talking. She had clinical terms for everyday discomforts. The upside was the fact that she could identify what she was feeling and verbalize it without a song and dance. Right to the point without a hedge or word of denial.

I picked up a fork and reached across the table to cut a section of her omelet before spearing the piece so I could hold it up to her mouth. She glanced at it, then at me with big, brown eyes that considered my offer to do half the work for her. With parted lips, she accepted, chewing slowly.

"What do you think her name means?" I cut another piece.

"It doesn't mean respite, that's for sure." She took the food.

"The core of my problem was in Damon's name."

"What about the other thing?" she asked. "You split again. That didn't even have a name."

"It might have come out if a bomb hadn't hit the building."

"Do you realize this means it can go on forever? You think you solve one split, and another pops up?"

"We didn't solve Damon with the deployment. Come on." I waved another forkful at her. "Eat. Don't make me do the plane and the hangar."

Ruefully, she opened her mouth and ate. After she swallowed, she said, "I'm glad I took it. Instead of you."

"I'm not." I pushed the half-eaten omelet around to get a better angle. "I didn't want this for you. And we could have handled it if it was me."

"I can handle it."

As I fed her the last of her breakfast, I had no doubt she could manage at least as well as I had. I was worried about my ability to handle being the sane one.

"I'm going to kill Ronin," she said.

"He thinks he's doing the world a favor." I put the fork down and put my plate in front of me. Dark spots had formed under the egg sandwich. "Fucking dangerous, that attitude."

I took a bite. It was salty and tasteless at the same time. I was starving. This thing was going down in two bites.

"I don't care if it works half the time," she said. "I want to destroy every one of those syringes."

"They'll just send more." I finished the sandwich with one last bite.

"I'm bringing it down." Her voice was determined, and a new fire lit up her face. "If it's the last thing I do, I'm ignoring the NDA and bringing it down."

The wind was picking up. Sand ticked against the windows like sleet. They could prosecute her for destroying property or revealing trade secrets. This Greyson was impulsive and action-oriented. This wasn't a side of her that thought through consequences. I had to do that for her.

"If you do," I said, "if you do anything to lose your access to Blackthorne's data, you won't have a case. They'll just hide."

"I don't care."

"And if they have a fix, you'll never get it."

"There's no fix. Nothing short of a completely accurate recreation of past trauma."

"You don't know that."

"I *do*."

"Damn it, Greyson." The force of my voice was raised,

but the volume was as low as I could make it. "You need to bend a little."

"I'm bent near breaking." She took her napkin off her lap and tossed it on the table. "I'm going to work."

I stood with her, blocking her way. "Don't do anything reckless. Please."

"I won't."

"Promise me."

"I won't do anything reckless." She had mischief on her mind. Worse, it was mischief with a purpose. "Not today."

Chapter Eight

GREYSON

The wind whipped. The sand pelted my skin. I covered my mouth with a scarf to get into the building. I wanted Caden. I wanted to stay with him. He soothed my need to be in motion. Without him, I was bigger than my skin. A balloon filled and filling faster, stretching thin as I tried to focus on getting into my office. I passed the storage room. Behind the coded door was a refrigerator stocked with prefilled syringes that, depending on the patient or the dose, delivered either madness or relief. All I had to do was go in there and smash them to pieces.

"Greyson!" Dana called.

Shocked out of my reverie, I waved and rushed to my office before closing the door behind me. Back to the window, I put the heels of my hands on the ledge and breathed as if it was my only job.

Wow. Okay. I could handle this. I was totally okay. A part of me could see how my desires and behaviors weren't consistent with rationality. I could see myself crumbling under them as if I was watching a movie.

Ronin opened the door.

"Get out."

He closed it. "You and Caden disappeared on me."

"Sorry." I shoved away from the ledge and pushed paper across my desk. "I have work to do. So, if that was all?"

He bent to see my downturned face. "I want to help you."

"I'm fine."

"Prove it."

PROVING it turned out to be harder than it seemed. My blood pressure and pulse gave me away.

"You really did a number on yourself," Ronin said as the Blackthorne nurse took the cuff off my arm.

"It's just stress."

The nurse showed herself out, and I put my jacket back on.

"I can't tell if you're consistent with other unprepped subjects taking a high dose unless you're honest with me."

"And how are those subjects doing now?"

He tightened his jaw for a moment. "Fine. We had some early testing in 2004, and they're fine."

He was minimizing or lying outright.

"So, there's no problem," I said.

"I didn't say that. We're working to develop a counter-treatment to undo the effects. Some of the subjects are at our complex in Texas."

"Some? Where are the rest?"

"We have a facility in Saudi."

I crossed my arms. "Long way from Abu Ghraib. That's where they're from, isn't it?"

"We're taking very good care of them."

"I'm sure that outside the destruction of their psyches, they're having a great time."

"You said you were fine."

He'd caught me in a fat lie.

"Touché."

He didn't rub it in. Had to give him that.

"I can't offer you a cure. But I can offer a little respite."

The name of my alternate rang like a bell. He didn't know. He couldn't know. It must have been the random use of the word that bent me enough to agree to a little of what he was offering.

Soo-hoo-soo-hoo-soo-hoo.

Sitting still in that little room was hard at first, but the breathing did calm me. I had to hand it to him.

Makeup in your eye.

Respite pushed against the barrier with a whisper. She showed me things I didn't want to see, and I had nothing to fight her with.

He said you looked like a raccoon.

She was showing me Jake in the front seat of his Chevy, smoking a clove cigarette. A sight and taste I hadn't remembered in years and didn't want to ever, ever think about again. He said something I couldn't hear over the wind. The picture flashed and disappeared, but Respite spoke clearly when she made me recall the scene.

Calm down, calm down. Jake told you to calm down.

A flicker of a Coke can. The hole at the top flashed with a flame inside it. Smoke.

Jake: It's done.

Jake's statement had cut through the fog. He was like Caden, deeply flawed and powerful beyond measure, as the flash from inside the Coke can lit his face.

Jake: He's got the cleanest fingers in the county.

This was before Scott had pushed me off the diving platform.

Respite whispered a correction. *You jumped.*

I'd jumped off that platform even though I was scared of heights. Why had I insisted he'd pushed me? Because it was easy to believe I'd had to save myself from his probing hands?

You jumped.

That was impossible, yet I knew it was true. He'd had his hands on me even when I'd said stop. They went between my legs, and I knew bad things were going to happen. I would resist it and like it and hate it, and bad things would happen.

You jumped to save him.

Respite was talking too damn much, and she could go fuck herself.

Chapter Nine

CADEN

Casualties of the sandstorm, civilian and military, started coming in as soon as I reported for duty. They'd been hit by flying garbage, gotten knocked off their feet, been found wandering and disoriented. People came in coughing up orange grit.

I shouldn't have left her. She wasn't herself. If something happened to her, I'd be responsible. If she went off half-cocked and broke every syringe they had, the consequences were on me. I'd let her go. Worse, she was splitting in two, and I couldn't do a damn thing about it. Couldn't even stay with her when she needed me. I'd abandoned my duty to her. All the times I'd walked out the door of our house in New York while carrying the weight of Damon on my shoulders, had she felt like this? When I'd deployed, had she been crushed by this level of failure?

I called her office repeatedly, like a desperate guy

she'd met at a party the night before. What a sad excuse for a man I was.

"*Shamal* can go on for days," Stoneface said as he plucked debris from an open wound in the shoulder of a little boy hit by a flying palm frond. "We're going to see a bunch of aspirated sand today." The boy cried out, and his mother soothed him. "Almost done, kid."

I bent over the freezer and retrieved an ice pop. Rosewater vanilla. I thought it tasted like a cold bottle of Chanel No. 5, but it kept the kids quiet. "If my wife comes in, I want to know about it, no matter where I am."

"For the hundredth time, yes, okay."

He spoke to the mother in choppy Arabic, telling her the disinfectant would sting. I unwrapped the popsicle. The boy's eyes lit up like Christmas trees, then filled with tears as the spray dehydrated cells and killed them off with a sting.

Nice bait and switch. Doctors are assholes.

I handed him the popsicle, and Stoneface got to stitching him up.

"Incoming!" Heartland shouted, bursting into the neighboring exam room with a gurney full of bleeding soldier.

We descended as another guy came through with his leg open at the thigh, screaming. These weren't sandstorm injuries.

"Get Boner!" I shouted when I saw the gray femoral fragments in the muscle.

"They booby-trapped it," the corporal said. "Fuckers. They put the bait and booby-trapped it."

I wasn't in the business of unraveling wartime who-did-what-to-whom. I had vitals to get and a trauma to treat.

With my powerlessness over Greyson tucked behind my carefully-built detachment, I got to work.

———————

FRESH out of the changing room, I started for the office. Surgery was done, and the wall between my personal life and the job on the table disintegrated. I was going to call Greyson repeatedly until she answered. From behind, I felt a vise grip on my arm pulling me in the opposite direction.

"I need you to stay calm." DeLeon said as she guided me down a hall with a sun-soaked window at the end.

"I'm calm."

"I didn't say *be* calm. I said *stay* calm."

The view through the window got clearer as we got closer. I could see the streaks and finger spots on the glass. By the time we stopped, the rest of the hall was dark and we were bathed in the light.

"Where's Wifey?"

"Why? Do you have one of her people again?"

"Answer the question."

"Is this what I'm staying calm about?"

"Major. You will answer the question."

Damn that bird on her collar. I had no interest in admitting the answer to her any more than I had in admitting it to myself.

"I don't know," I said.

"Okay. As long as she's not here."

"Why?"

"I don't want her hearing this from anyone else."

"If you wanted my attention—"

"That unit that just came in? The ones that were booby-trapped bloody?"

"Yeah?" She definitely had my attention.

"They were looking for the Al-Taqa Six."

"They found them?" I wasn't even finished before I knew I would have seen them if they'd been found or wired with C4. "Or... they were the bait?"

"Their dogtags were the bait, apparently. I couldn't get more than that. But this unit raided the house thinking they'd found them. They were moved. The scene was a mess, then once they tried to take the tags..."

"Boom."

"Blackthorne has ears everywhere." She put her hand on my arm. "She's going to find out. It should be from you."

"Thank you," I said, but it wasn't enough, so I repeated it. "Thank you."

"You have an early morning shift. Oh five hundred," she said. "I need you here. No excuses."

GREYSON and I were safe in her apartment with the windows shuttered against the storm. I'd given her a sedative, but that seemed to only make her agitation worse. Telling her about her brother would send her through the ceiling.

"Have you tried the circular breathing?"

"At work." She crossed from one side of the room to the other. "We did a session."

"Can you do it now?"

"I don't think I can."

"Why not?" I sat on the sofa and invited her to join me.

She sat. "I can't sit still for it." She got up. "There's so much I want to tell you, but it's hard to keep my thoughts together to do it." She cleared her throat and cringed against pain. "It's hard to stay in this room."

"What's hard about it?"

"I need somewhere to go. Some purpose, you know? Or it's so uncomfortable I can't think."

I got up and held her arms at the elbow, keeping her still. My gaze met hers. She looked like a caged animal. Frantic, panicked by her surroundings.

"Your purpose is to talk to me. That's your goal. Do you hear me?"

She swallowed. Nodded. A little of the frenzy drained away.

"Say it." I knew talking would hurt, and demanding it was unfair and sadistic, but it was for her own good. "Tell me what you're here to do."

"I don't think that's going to work."

"Say it anyway. You know it's true."

Deep breath. "I have to tell you everything."

"That's your purpose."

"That's my purpose."

"Now believe it."

I held her stare for a while, trying to catch the frenetic energy as she released it and redirect it back with confidence.

"This," she said. "This is me. Running and driving forward. It's not mania so much, because I don't feel all-powerful. I don't have an unrealistic idea of my own abilities. But there's this push. Like I have to advance some agenda even if it changes once I finish."

"Stay with me. Right here." I led her to the couch so she could sit as long as she was able.

"When you had this thing," she said, "when Damon was around, did you feel incomplete? Like not a whole person?"

"Yes. I didn't think of it that way. But yes."

I ran my fingers over the top of her hand. She was in so much pain. I knew that pain, yet she seemed the worse for it.

"I feel like Respite took half of me and hid it behind a screen." She tried to get up, but I held her hands in her lap and she stayed. "She wants to show me things, and Caden, I don't know what they are, but I don't want to see them. And this half of me is running while she's just waiting. I feel it. It's like a dead weight on me. How did you deal with it? How?"

I didn't have an answer that would satisfy myself or her.

"Don't let her own you. Don't let her take over."

"She's not trying to be me. She's trying to help me. That scares me more than anything."

"Why? What's going to happen if she helps you?"

"Then I'm alone with it. With something. I need her to stay, and I need her to stop. It's both and neither. I can't make her stop, and I can't make myself stay still."

Her brown eyes went glassy with a layer of tears, and her words bypassed her torn throat so she could speak in a breathy whisper. "If you took my arms and legs away, I'd know who I was. Take my eyes, my ears, I'd still be me. But my sanity?" She blinked, and the tears fell. "Who am I?"

I tried to hold her, but she pushed me away and stood.

"Even if I get this fixed," she continued, "I know it can happen. I can be broken. There's something wrong inside me. How will I ever be the same?"

I could barely hear her through the tears and the shredded throat. When I reached for her, she tried to get away, but I grabbed her and pulled her back onto the couch.

"Your job is to sit here."

"That's not a purpose."

"Yes, it is."

"It's not forward."

"You're exhausted." I wiped her tears, but there were so many I couldn't dry her face completely.

"I can't sleep. Not when I'm..." She hitched a breath. "Not when I'm this way."

"The other one sleeps. Respite. And I think I know how to get her out."

"No." She shot up. "No, I don't want her. I'll be this until we figure it out." Pacing. Again. To the closed window. To the door.

I jumped up and put my hand on the door to keep it closed. Her lips twisted into a snarl.

"Get out of my way."

"I'll tie you down whether you like it or not." I pushed her against the door, hovering over her so closely I was a cage.

"You can't control me, so you threaten me?"

"Keep feeling sorry for yourself, and they won't be threats."

She pushed me away, and I pushed her back.

"You're crossing the line, Caden."

"Oh, fuck the line." I took her chin and made her look at me. "Fuck all the lines. Draw me a million fucking lines, and I'll cross all of them to get to you."

She swallowed against the pulse inside my wrist.

"Let me go," she whispered.

"Let me help you."

"Help what? I can't take this. I can't take another minute. I can't live in my own head anymore. I don't know who I am or what I think. I'm at my limit. I can't take it. I'll do anything to make it stop."

"Let me help you." My hand slid down to her chest. I held her in place gently, letting her know I was there without trapping her.

"Help me what? Tell me what, and I'll do it."

What did I want her to do? I was at as much of a loss as she was. I'd have done anything for her, but there was nothing to do. "You need to rest. We need to relieve the pressure from the other... Respite. Let her through. Let her help you."

"I don't want to."

"You're never going to get on the other side of this unless you do."

"How do you know that?"

"You just told me. You just said she'd disappear when she was done."

She pressed her mouth shut and averted her gaze from mine. She didn't have an answer.

"I know how to switch it," I said. "Damon was triggered by the sunset. The darkness. You have a different trigger."

When she looked at me, she was open and curious. "What is it?"

I couldn't help but smirk. "Orgasm."

"Only you would come up with that."

"Hardly. It was you." I unbuttoned her fly with a twist of my fingers. "You flip when you come."

She relaxed her shoulders, moving her head to the side as if she was considering the proposal. "I think you're wrong, but it won't hurt to try."

"That's my girl."

I backed up to give her space, moving aside so we could go deeper into the room, but I'd underestimated her again.

She spun around, opened the door, and walked out.

When my wife decided to self-destruct, she went at it the same way she went at everything—with grit and resolve. I'd expected that. I hadn't expected the speed.

She didn't go out. She went *up*, and even if she didn't know what she was doing, I did.

She didn't want a rest. She wanted this to end. She was going to recreate her fear and face it.

The stairs were outside the building. Drifts of sand had accumulated in the corners. She took the steps two at a time, using the bannister to hoist herself up faster, with me at her heels.

"Greyson!" My voice sounded like wind.

My view of her narrowed and folded as she stepped from the stairs onto the roof. The wind was more powerful up there, and it came from every direction. She had her knees bent and her elbow crooked over her face.

I grabbed her free arm. "What the fuck are you doing?"

She didn't answer. She stretched herself toward the edge of the building. I pulled her to me.

"I am not going to let you hurt yourself."

She twisted away but didn't run. She was out of her mind. Free of sound judgment. Listening to voices that wanted her to act without thinking. I knew those voices. They'd told me to punch a wall to break my wrist. They'd made me jerk my dick bloody. They weren't foreign intruders but the voices that we dismissed when we were in our right minds.

We were both compelled to do something, anything, but we were being pushed in opposite directions. The difference between us was that for the moment, I was sane.

That was the final realization. I put my love away. My compassion took a back seat to professional detachment. There were things that had to be done to save her. She had to be stabilized before she could be cured.

She got two steps toward the edge of the building, crouching against the push of the storm.

The wind slowed her down enough to catch. I grabbed her arm, then her waist, pulling her back against my chest. We fell to our knees with her writhing and me trying to get control of her.

"Caden," she said without reprimand. It was a call to her husband.

I put my hand into her waistband. "Let me, Greyson! Help me!"

She bent over, and I followed, jamming my hand all the way down until I felt where she was soft and wet. My weight held her down.

"I don't want Respite." Her voice was nearly lost in the wind, but I was close enough to hear.

"You need it." I found her clit. It was hard and slick. My hand could barely move against the weight of our bodies and the restriction of her clothes. "Let me in. You want it too."

"Don't hurt me."

I froze, processing the new request. My detachment shattered.

She was mine to protect. Mine to heal and love. No one should hurt her. Ever. Not me. Not her. No one should ever breach her wishes with their own.

"I won't."

I rubbed her, and she bucked under me. My cock pushed against her ass, raging to get inside her. Her legs relaxed and opened a little. My hand went lower and deeper, fingering her opening before finding her clit again. Flicking, squeezing, circling, until her hips gyrated under me and the sound of the wind seemed to move farther away.

The pressure to come from just the grinding motion was immense, especially when she pushed back against me to get her hand under her. It joined mine between her legs, directing my movements.

The last time I'd made her come when she was a woman in motion, she'd been on top, commanding the situation. I let her have control again, moving my hand with hers as we grinded against each other. Sand skittered across her cheeks and lips. Her face was lost in pleasure. Magnificent and mine alone.

"God, baby," I growled. "You're making me want to come."

She answered with parted lips and a stiffened spine. The sight of her orgasm sent me over the edge, and I came with her, blowing it into my shorts like an adolescent.

We balled up on the roof, breathing against each other while the wind whipped around us. Who was under me? When she spoke, what would she say? Would it be active Greyson telling me how wrong I was about her trigger? Or would it be Respite, whose name was a lie?

I knew before she opened her eyes or spoke. I knew by the lack of tension in her joints and the easy rhythm in the rise and fall of her back. Getting up on my hands and knees, I observed her, and she opened her eyes, squinting against the flying sand.

"Respite?"

She smiled wanly. More awake than before. More aware and somehow more dangerous. "You're saying it wrong."

Part Two

RESPITE

Chapter Ten

RESPITE

Most people don't know when they're going to die, but I did.

I had an all-consuming drive—and it went backward.

When I was at the beginning, I was at the end. I'd have fulfilled my purpose, and past it, there was nothing but a void.

It didn't matter. My will to survive was nothing compared to the will to go back.

When Caden got off me, I got to my feet. I was wobbly because I couldn't pay attention to the act of standing. Every bit of energy went to remembering.

"Can you walk down?" He held me up by the waist.

I nodded, squeezing his hand. What a beautiful creature he was. With the orange sky behind him and his eyes squinting against the storm, he was deeply rooted in the world and all its troubles. He was a god causing the pain he cured.

"I can."

He led me to the steps, keeping his hands on me as if I had the will to run away.

I was grateful to him, but he wouldn't make me come again. Not until this was finished.

The screen flickered to life, and I was eighteen.

I COULD IDENTIFY two separate cricket sounds and tell the difference between a breeze from the west and a wind from the north. I was more sober than I had any business being. The happy, swoony feeling was gone, as was the sick swimmy feeling. My lucidity was painful.

Nighttime was a devil of clarity. All the doors open. Owls. Crickets. Birds. Scuttling in the bushes. Things breathing. Hearts beating. Somewhere. Anywhere. The cracking of nail polish being worried off sounded like a jackhammer in slow motion. The moon and stars were hidden behind a thick layer of clouds that caught the lights from the ground, diffused it, and sent it back as a shadowless mass.

The lights were off, and the engine clicked as it cooled. In the passenger seat of Jake's Chevy, I chipped my nails from solid purple to jagged gray.

Snick-snick-snick.

Waiting for my brother to get back, I congratulated myself when I got a big piece and brushed it off my skirt when it fell.

Snick-snick.

I got right back down to business. My full attention on

cracking the polish meant I could move forward without looking back. This project in the cacophony of the night kept me from turning my mind back in time. Kept me from thinking about the weird brokenness between my legs. The soreness that reminded me of my deep corruption. The thing that caused all the other things that...

Snick-snick-snick.

If I'd known where I was going, I could have run there. If I'd been avoiding something my whole life, I would have hurtled myself into it full force. But I'd been adrift. I had nothing to run to any more than I had anything to run from. Until now. Now I had something to run from, but it was everywhere. You can't escape if you're running in circles.

Snick-sni—

"Ow." My voice sounded alien, and when I put my finger in my mouth, it tasted of enamel and blood.

I opened the glove compartment. The light went on. I wasn't supposed to shine a light or make a sound, so I hurried to grab a Burger King napkin from the compartment before the light cut too much of the night.

I closed it softly. Maybe the shock of light woke up a part of my brain that had gotten used to the darkness. Maybe my corneas had a temporary burn. Maybe some higher power had something to say. I don't know why the picture of what was under the napkin was imprinted in my mind, but even with the return of dark and the bleeding under control, it remained.

BE ALL YOU CAN BE.

Jake had enlisted six months before and had only

been home a few days. He loved the military. The order. The routine. The challenges. Even the hierarchies.

ALL YOU CAN BE.

What was I?

Snick-snick-snick.

Was I who I had been yesterday? Or was I who I'd become in the past three hours?

YOU CAN BE.

I'd sneered at him when he came home, but he'd just smiled as if he knew something I didn't.

CAN BE,

I considered myself a pretty shrewd customer. A real cynic. I could sniff out falsehood. I knew PR when I saw it. "Be All You Can Be" was pure public relations magic, even to a girl who had made eyeliner into an art and wanted hair so dark it could take out a city block.

BE- *snick*-ALL- *snick*-YOU- *snick*-CAN- *snick*-BE.

But what could I be?

Could I live in a straight line?

Could I have forward motion?

Quickly, I opened the glove compartment, got out the pamphlet, and snapped it closed. I could barely see it, yet I had the pitch memorized. The front photo was deeply saturated in orange-and-yellow sunrise with the silhouette of cavalrymen marching, arms raised in command, every one a leader. In the rusty sky, a line of parachutes opened.

WE DO MORE BEFORE BREAKFAST THAN MOST PEOPLE DO ALL DAY.

Onward. I didn't have to look back if I was going

toward something. I wouldn't be blindsided by the things I'd done if I could just keep momentum.

The back had a business card clipped to it. The recruitment office on Shiloh Street. Lieutenant Barry Driggs. US Army.

Lieutenant Barry Driggs knew who he was and where he stood. He knew where he was going because the army told him so. The army pointed him in a direction and didn't let him look back. He was one of them. So was Jake. That was what he had been smiling about when he got home.

Escape. The hope of a beautiful escape into purpose.

The dome light snapped on as the driver's side door opened. Jake got in and closed the door before the dashboard beeped twice. He smelled of alcohol wipes and twenty hours without a shower.

"Hey." I tucked the pamphlet under my leg. "How did it go?"

"Uneventful." He cracked a can of Coke. It hissed as he sucked the bubbles off the lip. The diffused light hit his sculpted cheekbones and the scrub of hair growing on his chin.

"You had time to get something to drink?"

He handed it to me. "Finish it."

"Why?" I didn't like the sticky brown crap with an indefinable flavor.

"Just do it. For once, just do what you're told."

I used the spotted Burger King napkin to wipe the bubbles off the side. Jake circled his finger as if to say, "Move it along." I drank as much as I could before the buildup of carbonation stopped me. My brother tapped the steering wheel and stared out into the darkness.

"Are you all right?" I asked.

"Yeah. I'm fine."

"You don't seem fine."

"Drink up, punky."

I took a deep breath and drank as much as I could.

"I'm fine, but..." He paused for a shallow breath while I got the drink down to a third of a can. "I've been taking sniper courses. They make us think of them as targets. Not people. Like if we tell a part of ourselves that it's really a person, it poisons the part that does the shooting. But I don't know. I don't know if I can do it. After this, I don't know if I can lie to myself."

"Don't ruin your life because of me."

We looked at each other a long time. Condensation dripped onto my finger and slid along its length. Jake was my older brother. He'd given me noogies and made fun of my body when it started maturing, falling into silence on the subject when it was finished.

Now he was a man.

And me?

What did that make me?

I finished the remaining cola and handed him the can.

"What are you going to do?" he asked, reaching into his pocket and pulling out a used alcohol wipe. It had a faint streak of blood on it.

"Lie?" My headache started there, right when the alcohol wore off. At the moment I told the truth about lies.

He stuffed the wipe into the can until only a small triangle of white stuck out. "Smart."

"Do you think so?"

"Yeah. If anyone asks, tell them I picked you up at one thirty and took you home. Do you have a lighter?"

"Sure." I got out a pack of clove cigarettes and offered him one.

He took it and the black Bic. He lit us both, then touched the flame to the white triangle. When it caught, he shook the wipe down. Yellow light flickered from the little hole, replaced with acrid smoke.

"I'm sorry," I said. "I did ruin your life."

He cracked the window and blew the smoke out, coughing. "This shit's going to ruin me way before you do." He dragged again and choked. I laughed. "It's like smoking broken fucking glass."

I took a long pull before licking the clove flavor off my lips. "Yeah." I smiled, flicking my ash into the empty can. "Ruins the shit out of you."

BACK IN GREYSON'S SPACE, Caden sat me in a chair. He pressed his fingers to my wrist as if the answers were in my pulse. I smelled the smoke from the can mixing with the clove cigarette. Tasted the Christmas on my lips. He was with me, staring at me as if he was trying to understand me, but he never would. I was the memory of what I'd forgotten. I was the events during a drunken blackout. I was Greyson's darkness and the light that banished it.

"You're thready," he said. "You need to rest."

"All right." I wasn't tired. I was drained.

"And eat."

"Sure."

I closed my eyes, letting the room slip away, going backward to my brother's car as he parked it on a back road and told me to stay there. I was to sit in darkness and silence. I was to duck if someone came. I agreed to everything, submitting to culpability for something that I'd done but couldn't remember.

The pressure of the chair under me disappeared. Caden had taken me in his arms and was carrying me to the bed, where he laid me down and stroked my hair from my face.

"I'm going to fix this," he said.

I opened my eyes. Above me, he was a protective force that had no idea of the harm he could do. I wished I was worthy of him. I wished my sins were as unintentional as his.

"No," I said, "She and I are going to fix it."

Chapter Eleven

CADEN

Hours had passed with her narrating the sound of the leaves in the wind. I'd sat still for it when I could, but mostly I took her pulse and her temperature, looking for something to latch onto.

Solutions. I needed solutions, and all I had were problems.

I didn't know what Respite meant by fixing it, but if she was anything like Damon, she wasn't going to fix shit. She was going to fuck it up.

Phone lines were down. Neither of our cells had signal. I didn't have a car, and I couldn't carry her to the hospital. I still hadn't told her about Jake because I couldn't decide which one of her would take it worse. Respite, whose world seemed to circle around him? Or Greyson the Unpredictable?

If she were injured, I'd carry her back to New York if I had to. But I hadn't yet taken her to the hospital because I didn't want to put a dozen doctors between us. I didn't want to answer questions, and I didn't want her whisked away from me to some mental facility. Because they would. The army. Blackthorne. Someone would take her away.

Greyson had a few granola bars in the cabinets and a bruised apple on the counter. A half-eaten container of hummus and a round of pita that still had a day or two in it. I unwrapped a bar and sat on the edge of the bed.

"You have to eat."

Her eyes opened halfway, as if she wasn't committed to looking outside herself but for the first time in hours, she'd try.

"Respite," I said. It felt wrong to look at my wife and call her a different name, but she wasn't Greyson either.

"Hello, Caden." She glanced at the bar that poked out of its wrapping like a bloom, then back at me. As Respite, she exhibited an emotional flatness I associated with distraction. She was never fully present in the room with me, and it made me impatient to see my wife again.

"What kind of name is that?" I asked. "A little on the nose, don't you think?"

"She turned my name into her wish." She sat up, sliding her bottom back and leveraging against her right arm. The sheet fell down her body. I'd stripped her to her underwear, and I was glad I hadn't finished the job. I didn't want to look at those beautiful tits on another woman.

"So that's not your name?"

"No."

I pushed the granola bar at her. She took it reluctantly.

"What's your name then?"

"Something like that."

"Like Respite?"

She nodded and bit off the tiniest corner.

"But not?" I continued.

She shook her head. This new personality took years off Greyson's demeanor. There was something very knowing about her but something petulant and naïve as well.

"I don't know it yet, but I will." She bit off another corner and chewed with more attention than chewing deserved. "I'll know once I play the entire thing back."

I waited. Did she think I knew what she was talking about?

"Do you have water?" she asked.

"Sure."

As I filled a cup, I watched her in the reflection of a tiny mirror tile. Greyson in a black bra and rumpled sheets but not her. Not her at all. I'd married a woman, and there was a girl in the bed.

"Thank you," she said, taking the glass.

I pulled up a chair. "What's this about playing something back?"

She handed over the glass, then the half-eaten granola bar. "A thing that happened. The memory is deep, but I had eight kamikazes. So, it's there? I can get it out, but only one thing at a time, from the end. Like I have to unpack the box from the top?"

I heard what she said. The words were fine, but the tone wasn't Grey. It had question marks all over it. I couldn't blame her for not knowing which way was up. I didn't either. Couldn't tell how long this would take either. Was she unpacking a two-year-long event or a bad few minutes?

"When is the memory from? How old were you?"

"Eighteen."

"Where were you?" I kept my tone casual. I didn't want to freak her out. She seemed fragile.

"Um, Jake just pulled up to a... like a side back alley-ish thing? It's a lot of cinderblock and gray. Light industrial, maybe. It's really dark, and I'm glad about that."

I'd thought I knew what my wife was going through because I'd lived it with Damon. But Respite was different. She spoke about her alternate as if she was the same person. Past the emotional flatness, there was a soft compassion for the girl whose story she was telling. A forgiveness. Respite's tone confirmed she existed to help, not conquer.

"Also," Respite continued, "there's kind of a gross swimmy feeling, and my tongue tastes like burn."

"The eight kamikazes."

She may have heard me, but judging from how her gaze went blank, it didn't matter. "The crickets are really loud. I feel like they're going to give me away. It's cloudy, but the light pollution from town makes the clouds bright enough to see by. And Jake is mad. He gets out of the car. He's got big muscles on his arms. When he left for the army, he was skinny. Now he's like a man. He scares me?"

Again, the question at the end illustrated how

different she was. I wanted to shake her loose. It had been hours, and I wanted my wife back.

She put up with Damon for weeks.

"Why is he mad?" I asked.

"It's three thirty in the morning," she replied without looking at me. "He wants to know why the hell I haven't gone home. What's on my freak mind? He always called me a little punky freak. And then I cry so hard he stops being mad."

She went silent.

"Respite?"

"When Jake gets out of the car, the gravel crunches under his feet. He's not wearing the boots he came home in. He's wearing his old Adidas while he's on leave, but he keeps his dog tags on. He leaves the car door open. The dashboard's beeping, and his lights are on."

She'd started from the beginning, adding new details but going no further back.

"Why is he there?" I asked.

"He's saying, 'Oh, fuck, Grey. Fucking fuck. Where?' and I point at a dark place behind the building. Jake goes, but I sit sideways in the car with the door open. I take the keys out and turn off the lights so the beeping stops. I wait a long time."

"What's happening, Greyson?" I called her by her real name because she wasn't respite any more than I was a back rub.

"There's a break in the clouds, and I can see some stars through it."

"Greyson." I try not to growl and fail.

"When I rub my thumbnail, I feel a place where the polish is flaking."

She was rubbing her thumbnail as if she was there, wherever *there* was. She was infuriating, making no effort whatsoever to dig out of this. She was just sliding into the details of a memory that could go nowhere and not answering the relevant questions.

She was about to talk again. She opened her mouth to reminisce about the light reflecting off the sky or some bullshit. I didn't want to hear it. Not another word.

I took her by the shoulders and shook her. "Listen to me!"

She focused on me for the length of fingers snapping. For that moment, she was herself. It was like taking a rib spreader out and putting the thorax back in its place. It all fit.

"Where are you?"

Before I even finished my sentence, she was gone. Heart, lungs, ribs—taken apart. Insides outside.

I was bereft. My body was inside out. I was the one with parts out of place.

"He's gone a long time," she said. "The crickets pause enough to let the sound of the rustling leaves through."

"No, no, look at me."

"I'm hungry."

"Okay, I'll—"

"I can hear my stomach rumbling in the pause."

"Stop!"

She did. I thought I'd be relieved, but her silence wasn't a refocus of her attention. She was deep inside herself and not bothering to tell me what was happening. This was worse.

My watch beeped, cutting my thoughts like a scalpel.

I had to report for duty in half an hour.

"Grey, listen, if you're in there. Listen."

I lifted her chin until she faced me. With my other hand, I moved my finger across her field of vision, left to right and back again. Her eyes did not follow.

"Jesus, baby, what's happening?"

My watch beeped. So close to her ear, yet she didn't move a muscle.

"I have to report for duty in half an hour. Talk to me. Tell me what to do."

The watch stopped. Like the silence of the crickets, it opened the door to heartbeats and breaths.

"Greyson."

Twenty-eight minutes to report, and if you're not ten minutes early, you're late.

"Grey*son*."

No answer, but her lips were puckered in my fingers. I smashed my mouth on hers. The woman in my hands felt like her. My tongue fit between her teeth just the same. She tasted like my wife. But she didn't respond. I pulled my lips away but held her head still. I was torn between staying with her and reporting for duty. The hospital needed me. The army needed me, and I'd made commitments.

"Talk to me," I said.

"I beg him not to leave me."

"I won't leave you."

"He says he never will."

"I won't. Ever."

"He's my brother, and we're all we have."

"We're all we have."

Did she hear me? Did she understand? Was I even talking to her? Or was I reminding myself of what was important?

Her eyes focused and found mine. I let her jaw go. She was my wife again. Partly, at least. She was still soft and docile, but she didn't seem as young or fragile. "Caden."

"Yes?"

"That part? It's over. I remembered everything I had to."

"Everything?"

"Everything that was there. I feel the things before bubbling up."

"Are you all right?"

"I didn't know you back then. It's weird to think there was a time in my life without you."

"I was there."

Her brow knotted, and she sat perfectly still, as if breathing and remembering couldn't coexist. Finally, her eyes met mine and she spoke. "I don't remember that."

She took memories and facts very seriously.

"Always. We were a promise the Universe made before we were born."

She looked away but not back inside herself. "I don't know if I felt it."

"You don't need to feel it to make it true." I gathered her hands in mine and laid them in her lap. "I knew it the first time I saw your face. You were a promise kept. I knew that if I let you go, I'd be breaking something bigger than me."

She slid her hands out of mine and around them until my palms were on her bare thighs. Pressing my thumbs against the insides, I pushed them open a few inches until I could see the damp crotch of her underwear.

"What do you want?" I asked, stiffening for her.

"You."

I saw my watch against her leg. Twenty-seven minutes. I was going to have to walk a quarter mile in a storm to get to the hospital. I had to leave... or not. I could smell the tang of her cunt, and the minutes were ticking by. I spread her legs farther apart.

There was another issue: an orgasm would bring back the other Greyson.

"I have to report."

"Okay." She lay back, legs still open, the fabric of her underpants creased in the center where moisture made them stick.

She was going to get herself off. If I reported, I'd come back to an empty apartment. She'd be somewhere in Baghdad, walking toward some purpose she made up just to give herself forward motion. We'd be separated again, and I'd have no control of the situation.

That was not acceptable. The US Army was going to have to deal with my absence.

Leaning over her, I hooked my fingers in her underwear. "Pick up your butt." I slid them off her and balled them in my fist. "Bra off."

She unhooked the front and wiggled out of the bra. I took it. Her nipples were pointed straight at me, hard and tight, a blush spreading across her face and neck. She closed her legs.

This personality had taken the shame Greyson never admitted to. It was more arousing than I'd ever imagined.

Grabbing her ankles, I pivoted her until she was lined up with the direction of the bed. The headboard was made of cheap metal piping painted white.

"Are you going?" she asked, getting up on her elbows.

"Not right now." I stood over her with her damp underwear in my fist. "Grab the headboard."

"You can't be late."

"Do it, or you're getting the spanking of your life."

She did it, lying back with her knees straight as a diver in a pike, the areas of pink shame growing across her skin. I let her feel my eyes all over her, lingering on her tits as they rose and fell with her breathy discomfort. The pleasure I got from her indignity brought a rumble of my own shame, but I ignored it. I had a purpose here.

Stroking her legs, I said, "What do you remember about us?"

"That I love you."

"About sex."

"Nothing."

"Nothing? Do you remember the spankings?"

Eyes wide with shock, lips parted. The idea shocked her.

"So, you don't?"

"No!"

"What about pain?"

"It hurts?"

She was my wife, but she was different. What had

Greyson gone through with Damon? Had it been anything like this? Had it felt just short of infidelity, or had it gone over the line?

I put a knee on the bed and pressed her inner wrists together. "You like it." I wrapped her black bra straps around her pretty elbows. "I'm going to tie you to the bed."

"Why?"

"So you don't run away."

I tied her elbows to the bed, letting her hands clutch the bars. Her big, brown eyes watched me. She was nervous, aroused, ashamed.

"I won't," she said. "I promise."

Standing to observe my handiwork, I lingered over the lines of her body. She was magnificent. I wanted to mark her with my name and drive her to the edge of reality, but I couldn't. Not yet.

You can still make it to the hospital.

I could. But I couldn't leave her tied up for ten hours, and I couldn't leave her untied alone to switch back to a woman on a mission, any mission as long as it took her forward. No. This was the right thing. Shirking duty went against every fiber of my being—except the ones that prioritized Greyson. Those fibers far outnumbered the dutiful ones.

"Do you remember the last time I fucked you?" I asked, standing over her.

"No."

"Right before, you were soft and detached like this. Were you remembering things?"

"I think so. Scott. At the pool."

"HAVE I EVER FUCKED YOU, RESPITE?" I ran my hands over her body. With her knees still together, she was strung tight, humming when plucked.

"I don't... no, I guess."

Kneeling on the bed, I teased her knees apart and up until I could see her glistening pink cunt.

"Let me tell you how it's going to go then." Gently, I ran my finger between her legs. "I'm going to taste you. You're going to come in my mouth, and if I'm right, you're going to flip. I have to talk to Greyson."

"But I have to *remember*." She tried to sit up, stretching the bra straps against the cheap piping. "She can't remember."

"Remembering can wait."

"No. It can't."

I slid two fingers inside her, and she gasped. "It will wait. I need to talk to my wife."

"I won't come," she said. "I just won't, and you can't make me."

"Is that a dare?"

Stretching to face me, she spoke through clenched teeth. "It's a fact."

My wife was my wife no matter which side of her personality was on display, and when she decided what she wanted—or didn't—that was the last of it.

"Challenge accepted."

I got up and undressed. She watched as piece by piece, I stripped my uniform. Each article of clothing I took off made it less likely I'd report for duty. Each badge and buckle laid itself down in service to my wife until I crawled between her legs, fully naked.

I kissed and licked inside her thighs until she was a writhing mess.

"I'm not going to come," she said. "I can feel the next memory coming."

"Remember later."

I kissed her clit, and she made a breathy *huh*. I laid my tongue on it, warming it, feeling its swollen resistance. I pressed her legs apart as far as they'd go and sucked gently on her nub before running my tongue down to her entrance. She tasted like liquid heat. Like passion. She tasted like connection.

I looked up. Her mound was in the foreground, then the peaks of her breasts, and farthest away, the bottom of her chin as she arched her neck.

"You're going to come now."

"We're calling Jake on a payphone. The quarters won't go in. There's gum in the slot."

"Oh, no, you don't."

"We pick at the gum, but it's hard to see in the dark and through tears."

I sucked her clit in earnest, and she cried out in pleasure. Three fingers inside her. Another cry, then...

"The four is stuck, so we dial wrong! Oh, God. God! We start over. We have to stop crying. We can't think. It's so fucked up. What's happening? We dig in the slot for the quarter! I'm not coming."

"Yes, you are." I sucked, licked, tickled, hooked my

finger inside her to rub the bundle of nerves inside.

"Four-five-four-nine-oh-three-two was the line in his room. Four-five... no, you don't."

Yes, I do.

I toyed with her asshole, circled her G-spot, sucked her clit.

"Pick up, Jake." Her voice was lower, less demanding. I was losing her. "Pick up. We don't know what to do."

I got on my knees and yanked her hips up so I could angle my cock to meet her.

"He answered! Jake! Jake. We need you!"

I entered deep and hard, and she gasped. Her body arched under me as I fucked her.

"Come, Respite."

"He sounds sleepy and pissed off. He's asking where we are. We don't want to tell him because we said we were at Anna's."

"I feel you. You're almost there."

She wasn't the only one. If I kept fucking her like this, I was going to need a five-minute boner break. I buried myself, pushing my body against her clit. Her face scrunched. So close. She was so close.

"Don't tell Mom and Dad..." She was there. I knew that face. "We're at the Red Spot."

She elongated the O and came as if it was the last vowel she'd ever utter. I released and came with her.

With Respite.

We're at the Red Spot.

Respite.

Red Spot.

Her name was a slurring of Red Spot.

I knew why Respite didn't keep the promise of her name. She was the reminder of a night eight kamikazes had hidden.

"Get off me," my wife growled.

"Welcome back."

"YOU'RE GOING AWOL?"

She'd gotten up like a shot the moment I untied her.

"I'm not leaving you."

She was already getting into her pants as if she was late for an appointment with the president. "I don't need a babysitter."

This woman was impossible. Both personalities tested what little patience I had.

"You need to stop long enough to listen."

"I can talk and move at the same time. First we have to talk about what's going on with you."

"With *me*?"

"Caden doesn't go AWOL." She pulled a clean shirt over her head. No bra. "Caden shows up." She stepped into a shoe. No sock. "You'd better get in before they court-martial you."

"I am showing up. I'm showing up for you. Listen. We can beat this if we make a plan. I can't keep going without your agreement."

"To what? Let you spend five years in Leavenworth? I won't be party to that."

"We need to hole up here and let Respite finish. Go backward far enough until she finds out what you're running away from."

"I'm not running away. I'm living my life."

I'd assumed I'd have a minute to talk to her, but I didn't. She went for the door. I leapt off the bed and stood between her and the exit.

"I'm tired of trying to talk sense into you," I said.

"Then this is the perfect opportunity to stop talking."

"This? The way you're acting? This is not you."

"Who is it then? Because this is the real me. The other one is a shadow of me. Maybe a subset of things I haven't done. Or have done. Or the bits I don't like… or traits I don't use… the waste all bundled up and shoved into the light. But she's not me."

"When I had this, I felt like one of me was real and one was an intruder too. But that wasn't it, and you know it."

"You're you, and I'm me."

"Meaning?"

I knew what she'd meant, but I thought she'd backpedal. Soft-shoe it. Say she was sorry or pretend she was talking hypothetically.

No such luck.

"Let me spell it out," she said. "You were always unstable. You were a psychopathology study waiting to happen. The moral rigidity with the personal impulsivity? The trauma denial? The detachment? The way you joyfully cut people open?"

"That's enough!"

"Did you start fires when you were a kid and forget to tell me?"

"I see what you're trying to do."

"Did you dissect your dog?"

"Yeah. I jerked off into the open carcass of my dead fucking dog. But I never, ever fucking said shit to you like you just said to me."

She folded her arms over her chest, inspecting the floor with her mouth pushed to one side of her face. She was cowed for a few seconds before she set her jaw and stared right at me. "Deal with it."

She put her jacket on, which she should have done before the first time she tried to leave, but she literally didn't know whether she was coming or going.

"I'm not going to turn my back on you because you insulted me," I said.

"Everything just got really clear." She zipped her jacket, and I realized just how naked I was. "You're in my way. You've always been in my way. You're an obstruction I don't need."

"I need you. I need the woman who could listen and think. What I have now is two people, and neither of them has a fucking brain in their head."

"You didn't hear me."

"I heard you."

"You didn't. So, let me say it again. I. Don't. Need. You."

I knew better than to take her words personally. She wasn't herself. Anyone with an ounce of detachment could see that. But I'd used my last ounce listening to an old story about a nightclub. I had no armor left, and she was on the attack.

"You just proved you do," I snapped. "You just proved Respite is your filter. You're a real bitch without her."

"Sorry to step on your toes. Get your clothes on and get out."

She threw my pants at me. They unspooled in midair. Their full length landed against my naked body and collapsed onto the floor when I didn't catch them.

Was I just an obstacle? Did she feel nothing at all? Or did she feel plenty, none of it affection?

Her love was in there. It was permanent. A stain that couldn't be scrubbed out. It could be covered but never removed.

"What's the Red Spot?" I asked.

"The what?"

"The Red Spot. It's where Respite got her name."

She stopped long enough to register the way Red Spot fell right into Respite, then she snapped right to the issue at hand: getting away from me. "If I tell you, will you leave?"

"Yes."

She leaned on the arm of a chair and laid her hands flat on her thighs. "It was a club in Logan Heights. They took our fake IDs. They played the music I liked, and it was just a completely unexceptional cinderblock box."

"Did Jake go there?"

She answered with a derisive laugh. "Jakey wouldn't be caught dead at that freak show."

"What if I told you he did?"

"You'd be lying."

"Respite remembered."

"Then she's lying. Damon was unreliable. She's unreliable. She's manipulating you."

In a single unguarded moment, the creature in my wife's body looked at my dick. She shifted, as if feeling the sore dripping I'd left between her legs from a fuck she couldn't remember.

She felt something. Even if it was jealousy, it was something.

"If you won't go, that's fine." She slapped her thighs and stood. "I'm hungry."

I was sure she was telling the truth, but I also knew this side of her as well as I'd ever known anyone. Greyson never changed a subject without a greater goal in mind.

"Me too." I snapped up my pants.

"If we go to base chow, you can check in at the hospital."

Check in. As if I could just say hello and walk out. That wasn't going to work, but getting thrown out of her apartment wasn't sustainable either.

"Good idea. You can save me a seat."

"Deal. I'm going to the bathroom, then we can leave."

She went into the bathroom and closed the door behind her, trusting that I was a complete fucking idiot.

Chapter Twelve

GREYSON

The sand crackled against the narrow bathroom window, then stopped. It opened onto an air shaft that sometimes caught a burst of wind that spun into the funnel of the space, then petered out. I considered climbing out, but even if I could swallow my fear of heights, the door had no lock and the window squeaked when raised. He'd be in here like a shot.

Peeing was a chore because I had to sit still for it when I could have been on the way to base. I'd catch DeLeon, and she'd tell me what she knew about Jake, or she'd send me to someone she knew or whatever. But when I sat still, I had to think about what I was going to do with the information, and that just slowed me down even more.

I had the nagging feeling I was missing something. Convincing Caden to go to base to eat had been too easy. But I couldn't look back and take it apart. All I could do was get to the base and slip away while he got chewed out for being an hour late.

Maybe everything was just easy and I should have been thankful.

I washed up, checking myself in the mirror.

Stopping was mentally painful, but I had to figure out what I was looking at.

I didn't recognize myself. I looked the same but different. Like my own twin sister. How interesting. Was I different because of my expression? Was it the peeling off of weakness that left behind a cold mask? Or was my way of seeing different?

Thump-thump-thump.

Three hard, quick knocks turned me away. Not the bathroom door, but the apartment door. A voice from outside.

"Greyson? Are you in there?"

And then Caden joined me in the mirror. Still naked from the waist up, he burst in and put his hand over my mouth.

"Quiet." His breath was wet in my ear. I struggled, but he held me in a vise of bone and muscle.

Thump-thump.

"Greyson!"

It was Ronin. I didn't necessarily want to see Ronin any more than I wanted to see Caden in the mirror, trying to burn silence into me.

I didn't like being told what to do. I especially didn't like being held down and hushed.

"I want you to understand something," he murmured. "This is what they wanted. They want to create people without emotions. Better doctors and soldiers. We fell right into it. What you're going through seems right to you because you've had all your bad feelings moved over to some separate part of you. You're a surprise success story, and they want to bring you back to Blackthorne. They want to poke you and prod you, but they aren't interested in helping you."

I spit sharp syllables that added up to "Get off me!" into his hand while the pounding on the door continued.

Thump-thump.

"Stay still."

He had a fucking boner pushed against my ass. My pussy was still dripping his cum from fucking *her,* and he was erect all over again.

I hated that I wanted it. I hated how the painful constriction of his bare arms turned me on. I hated that the only thing that soothed my need to run out the door was his body. Stopping to go to the bathroom had been mentally painful, but stopping to fuck him? Not painful.

The thumping stopped, but he still held me. The sand ticked against the window. Silence reigned. We watched each other in the mirror, and the blue eyes I could always spin up into were just a color to me. No sky. No canopy. No bowl of protection. Just blue.

Since I'd taken the BiCam, I'd known something was wrong with me. I was sick with a mental flu. But a flu came with the assumption of recovery. It wasn't until I felt nothing in Caden's gaze that I knew I was broken.

And even in that knowledge, nothing changed. Caden could slow me down with sex, but he couldn't protect me or heal me. I was crowded with the need to push forward even though I knew my drive toward purpose was fake. It was a result of this brokenness. I still had to move.

It was as if my self-knowledge had been split from myself.

"I'm going to move my hand," Caden said. "If you scream and he's still there, you'll go with him and I won't be able to get you."

His palm lowered, leaving behind a chin wet with spit. He leveraged his arms on the counter. The pressure of his hips still pinned me to the sink.

"He's gone," I said.

"He's coming back," he whispered, "and he won't be alone next time."

"You don't know that or anything." I looked away. Opposing him was a knee-jerk reaction. I had to fight him. I didn't even know why.

"They're going to take you away, and they're going to lock you in a room. Maybe for a day. Maybe a week. Maybe I'll never see you again."

I'd already told him he didn't know that or anything, and he still didn't. But I knew plenty, and he was right. I'd be taken away.

What would I fight then? What would I push against?

"What's your plan?" I asked the man in the mirror.

"You need to remember, and we need to use the memory to fix this."

He must have said it at the exact right time because in the crack between how messed up my head was and what Ronin wanted out of me, I heard him.

"I don't want to."

"I know."

"I want to run."

"I know, baby. I know." He turned to kiss my cheek

When he looked back at the mirror, the protection of the sky was back in his clear blue eyes. For a second, I was home inside him again.

And then it was gone, and blue was just meaningless mutation in eye color.

My skin was too tight. My boundaries too close, and I expanded into a burst of tears.

No.

I was not crying. This was not the time. I took a tight breath through my nose, expanding against his chest.

"Tell me what to do," I said.

"Agree to remember."

"What if it doesn't work?"

"You'll get carted away, and I'll be court-martialed for desertion."

With Damon gone, it was easy to forget Caden had a deeply manipulative side. He was going to use his own decisions to direct me. He'd destroy his life to make sure I didn't destroy mine, which was noble, crazy, and calculating.

"Don't worry about me," he said, taking his hands off the counter so I could turn and face him. He must have been reading my mind. "I'll be fine. Remember for yourself. Do it for your own sanity. Not for me."

He leaned away, giving me more space. I could get to the door. I had shoes on already. All I had to do was *go*. The impulse formed and grew the longer I denied it.

"Invite her back," he said, eyes on mine as his hand

drifted down my shirt to the ridge of my waistband. "I'll stay here. She won't take over."

"It feels like she will."

He increased the downward pressure on my pants. "I know."

He did. He knew how painful it was to let the other take over, yet he wanted me to go there.

This was Caden. If I trusted anyone with my soul, it had to be him. I trusted him more than myself with my well-being. I'd forgotten that, but even in the mess of urges I was fighting, that one truth was clear.

I pushed his hand away. "I'll do it."

His lips tightened slightly, and one eyebrow twitched. "Go ahead then."

"You're staying to watch?"

"Hell yes."

Getting down to business, I put my hand down my pants and maneuvered to my wet pussy. It was sore and wet with more than my own juices, and I lost a bit of my arousal to a swirl of resistance and motion.

"How's that feel?" he asked.

"Freshly fucked." I started to yank my hand out, but he held it down.

"Remember how it was with Damon?"

"Fuck you."

He smirked and pulled my shirt up to kiss my breasts. I was wet and firm under my fingers but felt nothing. I stopped moving.

"Too pissed to come?"

"I think I'm scared."

He reached behind me to the medicine cabinet. "I bet

you are." He searched over my shoulder and took something off the shelf. "Let's see if we can distract you." Holding up a pair of eyebrow tweezers, he said, "Go on. Touch yourself."

The tweezers were angled at the ends, creating a sharp tip. He pinched them together in front of me.

"Lightly," he said. "Don't overdo it."

I did as he asked, giving myself a fistful of nothing as he pressed the two points against the skin over my left breast.

"I've wondered," he said, drawing the tweezers across, "which one of you likes the pain?"

The sting crackled along my body, humming down my spine and awakening the nerves under my fingers.

"I've been hoping it's this side of you. I'd hate to lose it."

Across my sternum, lightly perpendicular to the scar, and circling the nipple of my right breast. I gasped when he increased the pressure.

"Watch me."

I did, but he didn't look back. He was working the tweezers over me like an artist on a masterwork.

"Touch yourself just a little harder," he said. "How does it feel?"

"Better." I only had two syllables to give. Offering my body to him for his pleasure took the rest.

"You're so sexy and perfect. Your skin is rising where the hurt is. It's swelling like it wants to get closer to me."

"It does."

Harder than before, he pressed the two points over the tender flesh of my left breast, lifting his eyes to mine.

"Finger yourself while I mark you, and don't come until I finish."

"Okay."

"What do you say if you want me to stop?"

"Stop?"

"Very good. Begin."

I circled my clit as he drew a hard, hurtful line down to the nipple. The pleasure followed the double line of sharp pain as my skin broke just enough to scrape but not enough to bleed. I watched his face as he worked, the sweat gathering on his brow, the short breaths that told me he was as aroused as I was. When he went too hard, I yipped.

"Hush."

The command to hold it in sent me closer to orgasm.

"Are you almost done?"

He looked up and pushed the points hard against me. The pain was a shot of pleasure, but I was held back by the distracting noise in my brain. I didn't want to flip. I didn't want to go into the darkness. Into the nothingness. If he was almost done, I was going to fail.

"I'll let you know when I'm done."

He put the tweezers between his teeth and yanked my pants to midthigh. He opened his mouth enough to let the tweezers fall into his palm, as if he was in complete control of gravity.

"I want her to know who owns you. I need her to spread her legs when I tell her to so I can bring you back."

Fucking bitch. I hated her. I hated needing her, and I hated her fucking my husband.

"Hurt her," I whispered.

"I will." He took his pants down and released his cock.

"Tell me what you're going to do to her."

"I'm going to bend her over this sink and pull her hair back so she has to look at the mark."

"Yes."

He put the tweezers below my scar and pressed hard down my body.

"Fuck her in the ass before you bring me back. Make it hurt."

"I'm going to bury my cock in her asshole." He worked around the ministrations of my hand, drawing with pain on the place where my legs met. "I'm going to fuck that tight little hole until she cries. I'm going to pull her ass cheeks apart so I can go deeper. She's going to beg me to stop."

"Don't stop."

He tossed the tweezers on the counter. "I won't. Not until she gives up begging."

"I love you."

"Come now."

I hurled myself into the orgasm and darkness.

Chapter Thirteen

RESPITE

I couldn't remember in the darkness. Not clearly. Not with detail. Not without forgetting it immediately. I was in a deep, dark hole. Hopelessly ungrounded even as I was so deep I couldn't think about anything but getting out.

Then a tingle of consciousness. The sound of soft chatter and crickets. Night birds and his voice. His hand on my thigh and the desire that came with the unexpected touch.

I crawled out of the hole with the pleasure as my glue, sticking to it to pull myself out, and after a burst, the light came, and with it, the memories.

* * *

I COULDN'T MOVE my legs. My scalp was a thousand points of pain.

"Wake up," a voice said close to my ear. Caden. "Open your eyes."

Light budded in gray bursts, then got warmer. Lines formed.

Day fought with night. Caden's voice echoed another man's. The mental and the physical swirled together until I couldn't tell one from the other, until a real physical discomfort defined itself. I was being defiled. Hurt. My ass was being probed.

He jerked my hair. "I told you to open your eyes."

A slick finger violated my anus, and I made a noise that was half grunt, half squeak.

"I told her I'd fuck you in the ass, and I will if you don't come out and talk to me."

I opened my eyes. A bathroom. Caden behind me. A mirror.

"Good."

"Ow."

"You want another finger?"

"No. Please no."

"But I promised."

"Please."

"Look in the mirror. Look at your body."

I focused. The mirror over the sink reflected me from head to navel. Behind me, Caden was shirtless, pulling my hair to make me look up, his expression a cruel, dangerous fire.

My body was marked in hot, pink double lines. Spots of blood had broken out.

"What does it say?" he growled.

I didn't answer right away. I was too shocked. He

placed a second finger at my entrance, and I clamped down.

"Keep clenching. Just makes it tighter. What do the marks say?"

I blinked, clearing out the last of the distractions. "They say *HIS*."

"Who is he?"

"You."

He let my hair go. "That arrow points at your cunt. It's mine. When I say it's time to come again, you come. Do you understand?"

"Yes."

He slid his finger out of my ass and pulled up my pants. "I want to hear everything you remember."

We shifted position so he could wash his hands. His dick was hanging out of his pants, touching the edge of the counter as if it was looking for stimulation.

"She made you promise you'd have anal sex with me?"

He shook the water off his hands. "I promised I'd fuck you in the ass until you cried. That's a different thing."

"And you're not going to?"

"No."

Even after the invasion of his finger, I was grateful. "What else did she make you promise?"

"You don't want to find out." He wiped his hands on the towel. "But you have to cooperate." He pressed the white towel to my chest. It came back with a tiny spot of red. "And you have to let me take care of you."

He let me have the towel and washed his hands, watching me in the mirror.

"I can take care of you too." I brushed my hand along the hard rod of his dick. I wasn't surprised at how it felt as much as I had a very clear memory of being surprised. It ran through me like a gunshot, coming out the other side through a bigger hole.

"Not necessary." He snapped open the medicine cabinet and took out Neosporin and gauze.

"Someone told me it's painful if you don't get it."

"Someone was trying to get in your pants." He closed the cabinet door and let his hand stay there while he looked down as if deep in thought. "I forgot how young you seem."

"At least I'm not telling you to hurt anyone." I started to pull down my shirt, but he stopped me.

"Let me look at your abrasions, then you eat. Do you understand?"

"I can." I must have sounded confused because I wasn't answering his question.

"I DON'T KNOW if I can do this." I clutched the sides of the metal ladder so hard that even through my fingerless gloves, my hands hurt from the unbuffed steel edges. The thick treads of my heavy boots were good for staying on a ladder, not jumping from one.

I can.

The side of the building was so close my breath bounced off it. The fire ladder that led to the roof had a latch at the top that lowered it the final six feet. I hadn't unhooked it because I didn't think I'd be able to rehook it from the ground. I didn't want to leave a trail of actions and intentions.

Up or down, Grey.

I looked down. It wasn't that far. Worst case, if I landed wrong, my femur would get shoved into my pelvis.

Imagining the smashing bones and ripped muscle delayed me another thirty seconds. Then a bird chirped. I didn't know one bird from another, but what if it was a morning bird chirping to welcome the sun? I had once chance out, and it was down.

I can.

And I did.

The air whooshed in my ears, the fall of hair in front of my eyes stuck upward, and my skirt flew up, cooling the damp tear in the crotch of my tights.

I landed on my feet like a cat, legs bent, arms forward with my palms down, pausing to assess if the shot of pain in my hip was anything more than a momentary shock.

I did.

I can.

I ran to the phone, patting my pockets for a quarter. I was still wobbly but sobered by the jump and all that had preceded it. A headache was growing, my stomach tightened and flipped, and my mouth tasted like topsoil.

MY CHEST WAS EXPOSED and cooled with the astringent sting of antiseptic.

"What happened then?" Caden asked, patting a section of the S with wet gauze.

"We called Jake." I was lying on the bed with my back to the headboard and my shirt gathered over my breasts.

"I wish you'd remember forward." He put the gauze on the side table and dunked a half-stale pita in a container of hummus that had been in the back of my fridge. "Open."

I opened my mouth, and he placed the food into it.

"I'm getting full," I said as I chewed. He must have been feeding me for a while.

He pulled down my shirt. "Good."

When the phone rang on the other side of the room, Caden went from relaxed to rigid. It wasn't until then that I noticed the storm had subsided to a strong wind.

"They got the lines back up quickly," he said.

It rang again.

"Are you going to get that?" I asked. "Or should I?"

"I have it."

He was at the phone in two steps. Clear of the last memory, I could pay attention to the details of him. I watched the efficient grace of his body and its perfect proportion, heard the deep sonorous layers of his voice as he said, "How did you find me?"

He was near, but without his attention, I fell down the hole into a black-on-black square with his voice booming from the sky.

"I'm coming back."

He promised someone he was returning as the roof got closer.

"I'm not deserting."

Caden got farther away. The new memory loaded and flicked on like showtime in a movie theater; his last words were a whisper before the lights went down.

"I have to finish something."

OVERWHELMED WITH FEELINGS.

Fear.

Regret.

Anger.

Confusion.

Anxiety.

I paced the edges of the roof, corner to corner, the hole in my magenta tights growing with every step. The Red Spot closed at two. The music below was dead. No more Visage or Thompson Twins. No more dancing to The Cure by swaying my body and moving my hands in complex, geisha-like movements. The patrons gone. The employee section of the lot was all parallel white strokes. The line of cabs out front had drawn down to the final rider half an hour before.

Must have been three in the morning. I had to get out of there. I couldn't stay up on the roof like a princess in a tower. I was a sitting duck. A lame duck. A girl whose options were limited by fear.

I stood at the edge of the ladder and looked down. I could lower it from where I was but not from the ground.

How did I get up here?

He'd hitched me up so I could reach the bottom rung, which was six feet over the ground. Then at the top, he'd gone around me so he was up first and he could help me over.

I'd been impressed by that.

Stupid, stupid girl.

Now the bottom rungs were still six feet off the ground, and if I unhooked it from the top so the entire ladder slid down, I wouldn't be able to get it back up once I was on the ground.

I paced the roof counterclockwise so I wouldn't have to go past the back of the building, but I had to check. What if...

No!

"NO!"

I sat straight up in bed with a full bladder and a heart pounding as if I'd run a four-minute mile. The moon was full in the window of the darkened room. The digital clock's red numbers read 0200, and Caden was rushing to the bedside.

"Help!" I shouted.

He took me in his arms and held me. My impulse was to push him away, but something stronger surrendered, and I fell into him.

"Tighter," I said.

He wrapped himself snugly around me until I could barely breathe. I was anchored inside him. Not moving forward or back, he held me in the moment. I needed that. It was uncomfortable, but I needed it.

"What happened?" he asked.

I didn't answer because I didn't know yet. I let the protection of his embrace surround me and took in the details of the room. The chair with the little light had a book on it. The clock flipped to 0201. Our moonlight shadows made the shape of a face against the wall.

"You stopped talking," he said. "I thought you went to sleep."

"What was I saying?"

"You kept describing a roof. I assume it was the Red Spot."

I pushed him away. "I don't want this anymore."

"Want what?"

I threw off the sheets, ready to get out of bed, but I saw what I was wearing. Underwear and a T-shirt. I leaned back. Reaching behind me, I grabbed the bars of the headboard and spread my knees apart.

"What are you doing?" he asked, eyes on the damp fabric between my legs.

"You didn't come before," I said. "In the bathroom. How about now?"

"It's tempting," he said. "But no. Not yet."

His words were pretty definite, but his face wasn't. Neither was his body. His hand twitched as if he wanted to touch me so badly. Fingertips circling thumb. I imagined one inside me to the knuckle, then the web.

I took a hand off the headboard and laid it between my legs, groaning as soon as I touched myself.

He took my wrist and moved my hand away. "No, baby. You're not flipping back until you're done."

"I am done."

"On a rooftop? I don't think so."

The way he was leaning, I could see his erection.

"It's true."

He leaned over to speak softly in my ear. "If it was true, you'd be gone." I could practically feel the throb of his dick against the air in the room. "Why do you want to flip back so badly? Are you afraid of not existing?"

"No."

"What are you afraid of?"

My purpose was to not exist. To push back until I knew all there was to know. My voice would be silenced, and only then would I find peace. I was pregnant with the unknown, heavy and clumsy, waiting for the pain that was promised before the inevitable.

But somehow, in the anchor of his arms, I didn't want the pain. I didn't think I could stand it. If I could hide away in the darkness, maybe I could avoid it.

I didn't want to tell him. I wanted to convince him it didn't matter.

"Once I'm finished, something else will come."

His face was buried in my neck, but the weight of his body gave him away, getting heavier at the shoulders as if they drooped in despair. "I'll be with you if that happens."

He wasn't lying, but there was a touch of doubt in his voice.

Two quick knocks at the door interrupted.

"Don't get it," I said, afraid of losing the protection of his body over mine.

"I have to." He freed my wrist and got off me, exposing me to the curse of freedom. I could move. I could get up and move forward even as my mind craved backward.

Neither. I wanted nothing to do with it.

Caden leaned down to the floor to get something.

I put my hand between my legs, pressing against the damp fabric. Caden grabbed my wrist again. His belt was in his other hand.

I must have projected fear, because he said, "I'm not going to hurt you. Turn over."

Another knock.

"Wait downstairs!" he called, then pushed me a little.

I followed, getting on my stomach. He straddled me and put my hands over my head, through the bars of the headboard. I really thought he was going to fuck me away from all this.

Instead he put my inner wrists together.

"Who is it?"

"Time," he said, looping the belt around my wrists. "I'm buying you some time."

"It's tight."

"I know." He got up. "I won't be long."

I had to twist painfully to look at him as he put on his shirt.

"How long?"

"Before you can work your way out and get yourself off." He flung the sheet over me so I was covered. "Which you will not do." His voice was a little lower. A little clearer. Stating a fact, not a request. "Or I'm going to fuck your ass raw."

He stood over me for a second before walking to the door, then he turned with his hand on the knob, checking his work.

He opened the door partway, slipped through, and left me alone in my darkness.

Chapter Fourteen

CADEN

The storm had died a quiet death sometime in the night. The air was clear and still, as if it wanted to make up for the wrongs of the previous two days.

Ronin waved from the courtyard below.

If I never saw that asshole again, it would be too soon, but this wasn't about what I wanted. Nothing was anymore. I needed him and his sorry, unaccountable ass.

I took the stairs down to him. The only thing keeping Respite from turning back into Greyson too soon was a belt that wouldn't hold for long, but I couldn't invite Ronin in. I didn't want him to see her. Not in her underwear or fully clothed. I didn't want him saying a word or making a promise. Respite might fall for anything he said, and I couldn't physically restrain her in front of him.

"Doctor." Ronin offered his hand. I took it. "I hear you're AWOL?"

"You heard right."

"May I ask why?"

"No."

Ronin huffed a laugh and took a pack of Turkish cigarettes out of his breast pocket. He offered me one, and I declined.

"So," he said after lighting up. "You're going to make me beg you for the reason you called me at three in the morning? Or can I assume you finally decided to really help her?"

"Can you reverse it? Or is this just a pitch to take her to Saudi?"

He took a long drag of his cigarette and let out a shit-stinking ribbon of smoke. "There was never a need to reverse it. The breathing controls it for most people. For cases like you, who never should have gotten it? You showed us the cure."

"A recreation of trauma."

"You were the most successful subject we had until a building fell on you."

"What about Greyson? People who took too much, too fast, and broke."

"We're working on it. We're this close." He didn't bother holding up two fingers close together. He flicked an ash instead.

I thought I knew what was best for her. I assumed her cure started with us, together. But for a single moment, I couldn't tell if I was being irresponsible.

Was my first plan of action correct, or did I need to change it?

I couldn't decide, and that alone was uncomfortable.

"You have two people watching us across the

balcony." I changed the subject, pointing up at the veranda across the yard. While Respite was in her reverie, I'd noticed the café table outside the apartment door was occupied by two people playing cards at all times of day.

"Just making sure everything's all right," he said.

"And I thought you were in love with me."

"Only a little. You showed us the outer limits of what we could do."

"And Greyson?"

"She's showing us the limits of what we *should* do. Listen. I didn't want this for her or anyone. I want to fix it. Bring her in—"

"No." The decision came from my heart, unfiltered by doubt.

"—you report for duty—"

"Not happening."

"What do you want then?"

"I want food. Light food. Fruit. Yogurt."

"You're holing up?"

"And empty that apartment. I don't want to see another one of your goons up there."

"You're worried about *us*? There are going to be MPs with a battering ram at your door if you don't report for duty. DeLeon isn't covering for you much longer."

He was right. The clock was ticking. I was going from AWOL to desertion.

"Get me the food while you get me a car and a helicopter out of here."

He plucked the cigarette from his mouth mid-drag. "You are out of your fucking mind."

His gaze shifted suddenly, moving over my shoulder. I followed it.

Greyson was coming down the stairs.

Ronin and I exchanged a look.

"Grey?" I said.

"Hey." She had on sweatpants and a hoodie, and she was the sexiest woman alive. "Hi, Ronin."

"Hi." His voice cracked with youthful insecurity. He dropped his cigarette on the ground and stamped it out. "Hi, Grey."

What the fuck? He seemed totally disarmed.

I put my arm around my wife. She jammed her hands in her pockets.

"What did you need?" I asked her.

"Just got lonely upstairs."

The silence was so heavy and uncomfortable even the birds and crickets couldn't make a sound.

"So," Ronin finally said. "I'll work on that thing we talked about?"

That thing?

He'd never looked so guileless. Something had happened to him in the flash of a second, because the Ronin I knew had guile. Plenty of it.

"The food," I reminded him. "Light food."

His eyes on my wife. I wanted to gouge them out and cut the optic nerves. I wanted to do violence I'd never wanted to do before. I'd known Ronin for four years and hadn't seen him look at Greyson like that for three and a half. I snapped my fingers in front of his eyes, and he looked back at me.

"Was there something else?" he asked.

"You'll figure it out." I tightened my grip on Grey. I wasn't leaving her for a second. Not for a court-martial or anything.

Ronin smiled ruefully. "Bye, Grey."

"Bye, Ronin."

He walked to the other side of the courtyard, hunched over like a kid.

"Go on upstairs," I said. "I'll be right up."

"You all right?"

"Yeah." I pecked her lips quickly. "Don't touch anything you're not supposed to, you hear?"

She didn't answer. She just headed for the stairs. I ran to Ronin. He turned when he heard my footsteps behind him.

"What the fuck was that?" I asked.

"What are you talking about?"

We were the same height, so meeting his stare wasn't a show of force. Not initially. Not until he looked away like a submissive puppy giving way to the pack alpha.

"I know you can fight," I said. "I'm just a doctor. But I promise you... if you separate us, I will find a way to destroy you."

"Yeah. Okay." He tried to leave, but I grabbed his arm.

"Ronin."

"What?"

I looked at his face critically. The light wasn't great, but I could see everything I needed to. "You took the BiCam."

He shrugged as if he didn't want to admit guilt.

Ronin didn't have *guilt*.

"Why?"

He jerked his arm out of my grip. "Just back off."

"Seeing what it did to me wasn't enough? What it's doing to my wife?"

"He did it to prove it was safe."

Talking about himself in the third person was jarring enough. The tone of petulant resentment overshadowed even that.

"That if all the prep hadn't been done," he continued, "the breathing, the graduated dosages... everything... it could still be effective. He thought Greyson must be hiding something or she had PTSD she wasn't admitting. Or her dose was too big. So, he took it. He did a whole bunch of math, came up with just enough to crack him open, and took it because he was the only subject he trusted."

I respected his ability to do to himself what he did to other people. I respected his thoroughness. At least, I respected the guy who gave himself the BiCam. This man standing in front of me could have been anyone.

"What's your name?"

He smiled with that same rue. "My name is Abe Grey."

For the sin of taking part of her name and making her a piece of his sickness, I almost punched him in the face right there, but he kept talking.

"She has a man's name," he said, looking at the top of the steps. "Isn't that funny? Did you ever wonder why?"

"Her parents thought they were having a boy and kept the name."

"She tried to tell him not to go to Abu Ghraib.

Everything revolves around that moment, you know? When she said no to him and yes to you."

"On the landing pad?" I asked. "In Balad?"

Years before, Greyson had been caught between my marriage proposal and Ronin's offer to assist in Abu Ghraib. She'd chosen me, and after news of the torture in the prison had come out, she'd been horrified and relieved. I'd just been horrified. I knew she wouldn't have had anything to do with it.

He nodded. "If she'd come... if she'd been there, she would have saved him. She would have raised alarms. It all hinged on her. But she wasn't there, and he stayed in ABG. He tried to sort it out. Take the torture down a notch."

I was torn between feeling sorry for the guy and wanting to surgically remove his nuts for shouldering my wife with his sanity.

I was the only one allowed to do that.

He looked up at her apartment on the other side of the courtyard, eyes wide with adolescent adoration. "She looks the same as when he met her in basic."

They were about the same emotional age, these two, and that bothered me like a hot poker in the ass.

She was mine. At every stage of her life. Before she even knew she had a soul mate. Before she even desired one. Every facet of her personality and every spark of every neuron in her brain belonged to me. Birth to death.

Mine.

"Listen to me." I snapped my fingers in front of his face. He looked away from the light in her window and back at me. "You get me what I asked for."

"What did you ask for?"

What caused his flip? Not orgasms. Not the dark and the light. Was Ronin's split triggered by the sight of my wife? I hoped not, because he wasn't seeing her again. Not as Ronin or Abe Grey.

"Helicopter out. A Blackthorne bird. Don't make a deal with the army. Call me on my cell when you have it. I'll get you further instructions when I have them."

He bit his lower lip.

"Do it," I said. "Do it, or you're never going to know how to get back to normal."

Chapter Fifteen

RESPITE

I'd gotten out of the belt by twisting my hands. It had seemed impossible at first, but I stopped feeling the pain when the pressure to roll a memory got to be too much. The screen in my head was firing up. House lights down. Projector threaded. Curtain open.

The next part was going to hurt, and I didn't want to hurt.

So I went outside to talk to Caden and Ronin.

I was Caden's. I knew that. I knew we were married. I knew he was mine. But Ronin confused me. I'd met him in basic, and my memories started there before going backward. He was familiar in a way Caden wasn't.

Dismissed from the courtyard, I paced the apartment, twisting one hand in the other, singing songs in my head and giving words to details so I didn't have to think the things I didn't want to think.

Ronin had taken my virginity, her virginity—our virginity—but not really.

That had happened before. But not really.

It had happened in the depth of drunkenness, when my brain had been too scrambled to make sense of anything. It had wired the memory all wrong, then blocked it off because it was fucked up. It was all so fucked up. It took the scramble and just said, "Forget it."

And there, the crack appeared. Light shone through, blasting the screen white for a moment before it all started at the first moments of a very long memory.

"I LIKE THE PLIMSOULS TOO," he said, talking about the band, trying to be cool in front of the punk girl who was actually new wave.

I knew he had to have a name, but no matter how many times I replayed the scene, he never said it. Maybe our introduction had been the only utterance of it and it was before the roof. Maybe the music had been too loud to hear. In my mind, he was Bryan Adams. The furry blond hair he'd wrestled into some kind of conservative shape and the chambray shirt left my head playing "Summer of '69" on repeat.

"I meant the shoes," I said, jerking my chin at his blaringly white leather high-tops. "Plimsolls go good with jeans. Even stonewashed."

We were sitting on the edge of the Red Spot roof, legs dangling twenty feet in the air. The building had been a warehouse. Pretty tall for one story. He had little cuffs turned at the ends of his jeans. I hadn't noticed that inside the club.

"I'll try that." He smiled. He had a nice smile for a regular sort of guy.

I knew the type. They came around because the Red Spot was the closest club, or the only one open, but they belonged at McSweeny's or Bar None, where they played Huey Lewis and the News and served Heineken by the gallon.

"So, where'd you get that name?" he asked.

He'd asked my name, and I made something up because I didn't want to be boring or explain mundane things.

"Trouble?" I said. At the bar when I'd made up that name, I'd picked a maraschino cherry out of the bartender's tray, feeling quite satisfied with myself.

"Yeah. Where's a girl get a name like that?"

"I was born trouble."

"GREY," a voice cut through the memories. A deep voice from another time. A voice that came after I did things. A voice from after that night. "What's happening?"

"The cherry bursts on my tongue."

"You were on the roof a minute ago."

"It's sweet, and the skin gives way under my teeth. I like how he watches me eat it. I feel sexy. Like a woman."

His fingertips brushed my cheek to remove hair I hadn't felt. "Where are you now?"

"The roof of the Red Spot. He's there."

"Who?"

The projector stopped, and I snapped to attention.

Chapter Sixteen

CADEN

The morning after Ronin walked out of the courtyard as Abe Grey, a plan came together, but everything had to be right. A certain precision was required to get rid of this completely. When Damon retreated, I'd thought I was finished, but another Thing had come. A more dangerous, more destructive split. Only the perfect parallel situation had healed me, and I had to create that for her, or she might split again once Respite was done with her.

She was slouched in her chair, one foot braced on the table in front of her, stroking her lower lip even as she spoke, then suddenly, she snapped to attention, looking at me in a panic. "I can't."

I kneeled at her feet and cupped her face. She looked like a woman in unbearable pain.

"You can."

"Make me her again."

I couldn't. The answers were close. Whatever they

were, it felt as if the moments she was reliving were coming toward clarity. We didn't have time to flip back to Greyson, who would resist everything about this process.

Four thirty in the morning. I was calculating my next move when there was a knock at the door. I was so wrapped up in our little world I thought it was Ronin with the food or news of a helicopter.

"Hang on!" I called, then stood before my wife. "Give me your hands."

She gave them, trusting me like a foolish young girl. Like a prick, I took advantage of her trust and led her to the bed.

"Lie down."

She did, but when she saw what I had in my hands, she started to get up. I lowered myself onto her, letting my weight hold her.

"No!"

"It's for a minute."

I'd cut the pull strings off the blinds and fashioned them into a knot I could fasten quickly. I got her arms around the leg of the bed and had her tied in one move.

"Let me go!"

I leaned close to her face. "I'll untie you when I close the door. Then you're going to eat and you're going to finish this so I can have my wife back. Do you understand?"

"You're going to bring her back?" Her face was lit up with hope.

"Yes." I stood. Her body was relaxed, and her face had the beginnings of a smile. "But I want to be the one to do it."

"Thank you." She blinked, and tears fell on each side of her face.

I put my finger to my lips, and she nodded.

That was as good as it was going to get.

I answered the door, assuming it was Ronin. Who else would it be at this hour?

"Asshole Eyes," DeLeon hissed. "What the—"

I stepped out and shut the door behind me. "I'm sorry."

"I don't want your fucking apologies. You're fucking AWOL, and I can't cover for you."

"I know. Don't cover for me. It's not worth it."

She crossed her arms and leaned on the railing, looking me up and down as if taking inventory. There must have been a lot to see. I could only guess what I looked like to her. No sleep meant bloodshot eyes, periorbital swelling, and hyperpigmentation, skin that looked as if it was coming detached. I hadn't shaved. Had showered so quickly I hadn't washed my hair.

"You look like shit." She confirmed my thoughts. "Are you sick? If you're sick, they won't court-martial you."

"I'm not sick."

"So, what's the problem?"

"The problem."

I didn't say more because the problem was too deep, too wide, too complex to explain on a doorstep.

The problem was I couldn't leave Respite alone for too long or I'd walk in on Greyson, or more accurately, Greyson would burst out the door running.

The problem was, if I told her the problem, she'd

order me to bring my wife into the hospital and I'd lose control of the situation entirely.

The problem was I needed to get back inside before Respite got to the beginning of the story. I needed to hear it in fine detail so we could recreate it, have her face it, conquer it, and walk away. It was the only known cure, and I wasn't getting talked out of it or distracted away from it.

"Is it her brother?" she asked. "She's upset?"

"She's upset." I hadn't even told Greyson about Jake, but I was telling DeLeon the truth. Like an upturned apple cart, Greyson was upset. "Have they found him? Dead or alive?"

"No."

"Shit. No clues? No leads?"

"Not that I've heard. And every day that goes by? Gets less likely they will." She put her arms down. "I didn't take her for someone who'd collapse about this."

"You never know a person until they're in crisis."

She sighed and rubbed her eyes. "Okay." She dropped her hands, letting them slap against her thighs. "I owe you, Asshole, and I like Wifey. But my debt's paid once we go from AWOL to desertion."

"I'm not deserting."

"After a certain point, you don't get to decide that. And I'm sorry, I know you want to be with her and you have control issues, but you're going to have to give it up. You're getting court-martialed either way. You can either turn yourself in by oh eight hundred, three and a half hours, or I have to call the MPs on you."

With a dull, flat cadence and a volume barely enough

to be heard through the door, my wife's voice came from inside the apartment. She was remembering again.

"Thanks for the warning," I said, putting my hand on the knob. DeLeon was supposed to dismiss me, but we were past formality.

She raised an eyebrow as if I'd made a threat. Or maybe she'd heard Respite's voice from inside as she started reciting her memory again.

"If you run, they'll find you. They'll lock you away and shove the key up your ass."

"I understand."

She jerked her chin at the door, indicating Wifey, who needed me and whom I needed. "There are no conjugal visits in Leavenworth. Leave her alone now for a little while, or be separated for fifteen to twenty. Your call."

"Thank you," I said. "I mean it. I owe you one."

"See you in the morning?"

The evening prayers began, echoing over the walls of the city, an underlayer to Respite's recital. Because of language or physics, I couldn't understand either.

"Yes."

"Okay. Good." DeLeon started down the steps.

I watched her go, unwilling to open the door while she could hear my wife's voice relay a story about a boy on a club rooftop. She waved to me at the bottom. I waved back, turning my hand into a thumbs-up, promising I'd be there in the morning and almost believing it. She strode out of the courtyard, leaving the morning birds, the Arabic prayer chant, and the muffled tale of a young girl in trouble behind.

Chapter Seventeen

RESPITE

This part was too long. It started too early, on the roof with Plimsouls and plimsolls. The tension of going forward was stretching me thin. I felt as if I'd break in the middle. At the chest. The way a rubber band got translucent before a tiny heart-shaped hole appeared at the center of the thinnest point. It would snap sometime after I started anticipating it and before I expected it, stinging skin where the kinetic energy clapped against nerve endings.

But still, I pulled the rubber band because I had to. Forward was backward. If I stopped, I didn't know if I'd go back further to begin again. So, I had to tell the story even after sunlight blasted my face and the sounds of a prayer chant on the mosque's loudspeaker stopped being muffled by the door. I told the story through the folded darkness of the door closing and the *click-clack* of locks.

"I'm back," he said, sitting on the short table in front of me.

"Is everything okay?"

"Everything's fine. He was kissing you."

"There's a lot."

"Take your time."

THEN HE KISSED ME. He was sloppy, mouth too wide, tongue a whirligig around mine.

The music had stopped.

His hands were up my shirt.

All the people were gone.

I couldn't actually taste his tongue, and I was pretty sure he couldn't taste anything either.

How was I getting back to Lia's? Or was it Anna's? Dina, maybe? I'd lost track of the lies I'd had to tell my parents to stay out past midnight.

His hands were under my bra before I could say no. It was fine. It felt okay. I put my hands on his body. Under the chambray shirt, he was tight and muscular. This was okay.

I didn't go for a guy like this. He wasn't the right type, but the heaviness that settled between my legs was more demanding than my taste in men.

We rolled onto the surface of the roof. Drunk. Not caring about the dead leaves and dirt. The grit of tarpaper and the jutting roofing nails. Just doing the thing. His penis was rock hard under his jeans. That wasn't new to me. There had already been copped feels through pants and grinding in cars. But no one had ever done what he did next.

He unzipped his pants and pulled it out, then taking me by the wrist, he put my hand on it. I was too shocked to pull back and too drunk to consider the consequences.

"Stroke it nice."

His mouth was a sloppy whirligig again. The skin of his dick was soft and paper-thin, stretched over a hard core. He rolled on top, pinning my thighs under hard knees.

"Wait."

When I took my hand away, he put it back, pressing it against the head. "Wait for what? You feel so good."

"Just wait." It was all too fast. The world was spinning.

"Don't be like that."

Twisting. Trying to get up past the sickening, drunken spin of the earth. He pushed me back down, immobilizing my struggling body under him.

"Stop! Let me *go*!"

He reached under my skirt and, with a hard grab, ripped a hole in my hot pink tights. He was bigger and stronger. His dick was already out, and with two fingers that didn't tease or cajole, he wove past my underwear, and with two fingers—

Knock-knock.

Chapter Eighteen

CADEN

She sat on the edge of a worn chair, looking into the space between the imaginary horizon and the deepest part of her soul, filtering details through a wider and wider net. Her timeline jostled, putting the wrong dialogue in the wrong scene, moving events around like puzzle pieces that wouldn't fit right until everything landed in its place. She took hours to describe minutes with a young man who scared the shit out of me, but I listened carefully as the moon ran her course over the sky.

When my attention wavered, it went to remembering Ronin's schoolboy glances. I knew when a man wanted my wife, and though I'd been jealous and possessive when Ronin was around in the army, once we were civilians, he'd never made a sign that he had any interest in her.

Until she was this sweet, vulnerable version of herself

that I didn't recognize. Now his interest burned so hot I could feel it on me. He hadn't been interested in Greyson until she'd become this woman describing a boy's chambray shirt, the white buttons, the upturned collar.

Respite, to me, never seemed like Greyson. She seemed defenseless. She was talking about this guy on the roof with questions in her voice, and I knew he was going to take advantage of her. I knew he was going to do something she didn't want and my wife would come at him like a lion. This girl would describe it as if it was happening to someone else, which it was.

He ripped a hole in the crotch of her tights a dozen times before she put all the details in their slots. I was girded for a violation I wouldn't be able to avenge. I wouldn't even be able to get angry because it would scare her, and she needed me to keep my emotions in check.

I could do it only when I reminded myself that this girl was getting sent back where she'd come from. Respite was going to be reabsorbed, and Greyson was going to come back.

Again, her tights were ripped. Again, he pinned her and reached under her underwear with two fingers. She'd gotten this far so many times before finding a new detail to backtrack. My anger over his fingers was just as heavy, but it had been dulled smooth.

Knock-knock.

Her mouth went tight, and though her attention stayed inside herself, she was aware enough to stop talking.

"Wait here," I said.

"Yes."

"I'm not going to tie you up."

Her eyes met mine. I couldn't tell if she was surprised or if she wanted to be bound, but after the implication that she deserved pain, I was reluctant to do anything she might see as punishment.

"Just..." I stood. "Just don't bring Greyson back yet. We don't have time."

"Yes. I agree."

Why did she agree? When she was remembering, she didn't seem aware of time. I doubted she'd heard DeLeon's warnings.

"Good," I said, putting my finger to my lips.

I opened the door as far as the chain would let me, letting in the sound of crickets and the whoosh of pre-curfew traffic. The knocker was backlit by the building's floodlights.

It was Ronin with a box under his arm. He had a puppy dog look on his face, and even though I had never been a fan of the sneaky bastard, at least I'd always known exactly what kind of sneaky bastard I was dealing with.

I closed the door behind me and reached for the box. He stepped back. "No."

"No? What the fuck did you come here for then?"

"We should talk. All of us."

"All five of us?" I went for the box, but he twisted away.

"I want to see her."

"Why?"

175

"I want to make sure she's all right." He swallowed hard, glancing at the door, then back at me. "This stuff, it fucks with you."

"Tell me about it."

"Just one second," he said expectantly. "Then I'll go."

"Jesus," I said, "I bet you were a nice kid before the army fucked you up."

Her shriek came from the other side of the door. "Let me *go*!"

I should have gagged her. That was my first thought as Ronin's eyes met mine. Behind him, the two Blackthorne contractors at the café table shot up and ran around the linked verandas to get to us.

"Ro—" I started to explain, but he shoved the box into me, sending me off balance enough to push me out of the way so he could open the door.

We spilled in. Me. Ronin. The two Blackthorne agents.

My wife was twisting on the floor. "Caden! Help."

Ronin was ahead of me. He leaned down to her, and there was a moment of them truly seeing each other before she spoke.

"Only Caden."

I pushed him out of the way to kneel by her. "What happened?"

"I got out," she said to me in a quivering voice. "It was terrible. So bad."

"It's okay. I'm here now."

Arms free, she wrapped them around me as we crouched on the floor. Ronin and the agents cast a shadow over us as I rocked her. His posture was wider, and his face was harder. He'd flipped like a coin. The sincere boy had left, leaving behind the sneaky bastard I'd always known. Except... not. Without that sincerity or that deep well of caring for his friends, he was just plain untrustworthy.

Ronin turned to the two contractors. "Close the door on your way out."

They left, and Ronin put his attention back on us.

"Leave," I said. My wife was shaking in my arms, and he didn't need to see it. Her weakness wasn't his business.

"I'm going to our facility in Saudi," he said. "We're close—really close—to making this reversible. I want her to come."

"You're not separating us."

"Either I will, or the army will. You're AWOL. At least if she comes with me, she's in the hands of people who know what this is."

As soon as he left, I was getting her out of here. We were sitting ducks here, waiting to get picked off and pulled apart.

"She's in *my* hands," I said. "Just go."

"They're getting a warrant."

So this was how it was ending. With military police and a forced separation. And when they found her, what would they do? Nothing? Or would they deliver her to a black site run by her employer? We'd be at square one with the memory unfinished.

Greyson was in full Respite mode, staring in the half distance between herself and the floor, brushing her thumb against her lip, watching her life flash before her eyes. I didn't want to leave her, but I wasn't sure I had a choice. Surrendering meant separating. Going with Ronin meant we could both be trapped.

I could make a decision one way or the other. Six of one or half a dozen of the other. But I wouldn't decide alone. I wouldn't decide this for her or without her. She wasn't a child, and she wasn't my charge.

"Do I have until morning?" I asked.

"Maybe. We're arranging transport, but I don't know how long the army's going to take getting it together."

"Give us until then."

I'd let him think we were going with him, but that hadn't been decided. He'd leave his people at the door no matter what I said. Crouching in front of my wife, I tried to break her stare, but I didn't. She kept on seeing what she was seeing.

"Oh seven hundred," Ronin said. When he opened the door, blue floodlights blasted half of Greyson's face, narrowing the pupil. "You're doing the right thing. For her."

I ignored him. We had a few hours and no more. Maybe our last hours together.

"What you have," he said. "Between you two? I admire it. It's what we all wish for... that one perfect partner." He stood, unmoving in the doorway until I looked at him. He spoke before I had a chance to chase him out. "She made the right choice. You were the right choice."

"I know."

He nodded and left, cutting the light with a click. Her pupil dilated again, but she didn't move.

I needed Greyson back. She was hard to deal with, but she was the side I could make a decision with.

Watching Respite think, I couldn't flip her yet. She was close to her moment.

"Respite," I whispered, "what's happening?"

Her head jerked once, slightly and sharply to say no.

Kneeling in front of her, I took her hands. "Tell me."

Her brows knit.

"Please." I had nothing else. No demands. No strategies. No manipulations. I could only submit to the will of my wife's frailer half.

"He says…" She stopped, and I waited. And waited. "He says, 'You're wet.'"

The last thing I'd heard was her shout, "Let me go." It had progressed with whoever this guy was. Bryan Adams. Plimsolls. Chambray Shirt. I had to catch up without speaking or making assumptions, but God damn, it was hard when my heart was pounding with rage and the only person around to hurt was the one who had already suffered.

"He puts his fingers in deeper. All the way. I'm not prepared. It hurts."

I am not angry. Do not get angry.

"He does it hard. It hurts and…" Swallow. "Something breaks. I'm bleeding."

"Grey…" I wanted her to stop. She was going too fast. I wasn't ready.

"He says I'm wet. He… he says I want it. I say no." She was hopping between pieces of dialogue, one after the other, speeding up. "He hears me. I'm sure he hears me. But he pushes inside me and…"

Her face exploded into messy, open-mouthed, saliva-string sobs. I took her hand. She could stop now. She could leave it for tomorrow. The next day. Never.

"I come," she says around the sobs. "He makes me come. It happens so fast, and he calls me a... a slut."

I'd told myself I was ready, but I wasn't ready for shit.

I knew those orgasms.

I loved them.

I cherished every single one.

When she cried over the one he took, she was my wife again, and that orgasm was mine.

It was hers to give, but it was mine.

What was stolen from me had been ripped from her first.

I pulled her into my arms. My wife. She was vulnerable and weak. She was sensitive and broken. She had always been those things, but I hadn't loved all of them. I hadn't loved the vulnerability. I had only loved what was easy to love. Strength and tenacity. Bravery and power.

Now she was sobbing against my chest. Not a young girl. Not a separate person I wanted to banish, but an indispensable part of the woman I loved.

All of her.

I loved all of her.

I couldn't do more than hold her. I couldn't fix or change the past. All I could do was give her the one thing she needed, the only thing I had.

Me.

My time. My body. My love.

I didn't know how long I silently stroked her hair

while she cried. I didn't look at the clock. Didn't care about the outside world. She needed me, and I was fully present for her. All of her.

Eventually, she quieted. I didn't move or ask her if she was all right. I didn't call an end to my comfort so we could figure out our next move. I let her call the shots.

She nuzzled my neck, running her finger along the fold of my collar. "Caden?"

"Yes?"

She didn't answer in words but in a caress down my chest and a kiss to my jaw. I twisted to face her. The tears had dried up, leaving puffy eyes and red cheeks.

I got a handkerchief from my pocket and held it to her nose. "Blow."

She let me hold it as she cleared her nose. "Thank you."

"I'm sorry that happened to you. I'd like to find that guy and kill him."

She looked away, pushing herself off me. Her nipples were bumps under her shirt. I brushed my thumb along her lower lip. It was swollen from crying, pillow soft, vulnerable and yielding. She opened her mouth and took it, sucking with big, brown eyes looking up at me.

"Respite..."

"Call me Greyson. That's my name."

"Are we at the end?"

"That was the last memory."

Sliding down to the floor, she kneeled between my legs and kissed the erection under my pants. She wasn't clumsy, but she was coy.

When she was at the end of her story, she was

supposed to be done helping. She was supposed to be reabsorbed, and we'd find out if there was a new split or if Greyson would be whole again.

Neither was happening. This was more of the same with an added touch of sexual aggression.

I ran my fingers through her hair as she looked up at me. "Baby…"

"Let me. Then I'll be gone."

Believing her was a conscious choice.

Having been in my wife's shoes, I knew she couldn't be so aware of the next steps with such certainty. Having spent days on end listening to her story, I knew she wanted to avoid pain.

But what if the forced orgasm was the pain?

And what if she was right and this was over?

She might need sex to flip to Greyson for the last time, then we'd know where we were.

I helped her get my dick out. I was already throbbing for those lips.

She kissed off the drop of precum that had gathered at the tip and ran her tongue around the head, then down the shaft and up again, leaving me wet and wanting. I watched my cock disappear down her throat. Holding the base, she took increasing lengths until her nose was pressed against my stomach.

She sucked dick like my wife, that was for sure. I pushed into her, driving deep, and she took it. All of it. The last time we'd had sex, I'd been left unsatisfied. It wasn't long before the pressure was too much.

"I'm going to come, baby."

She popped off, chin shiny with spit. "Where?"

"Wherever you want."

She opened her mouth.

"Then take it all. Swallow it."

She impaled her face with my dick, stroking and sucking, opening her throat. I pumped my hips to her rhythm and exploded in her mouth. She took it all like a fucking champ, like Greyson always did. I stroked her hair away as she licked me clean until I was at half-mast.

"Do you feel better?" I asked.

"Yes."

"Good. Come up here."

When she stood, I slid off her pants and underwear, then I turned her around on my lap so her back was to me.

"Open up." I pulled her legs apart until they were draped on either side of my knees. "You're so fucking sexy. You give me so much." I pulled her shirt off and felt the hard, twisted pebbles of her nipples. She held my hand over one.

"Pinch it," she said, and I did, twisting until she leaned against me with a groan.

I could see her in profile against my shoulder. Parted lips. Eyes half-closed. Cheeks flushed.

"You like it."

"Hurt it."

I didn't expect this side of her would like pain, but when I pulled her nipple, she went taut with agony and pleasure. I pulled my knees apart, spreading hers. I reached down between her legs. So wet. Her arousal was getting me hard again.

"You want it to hurt?"

"Yes, please."

I flicked her swollen clit, and she twitched. "Don't move."

"Okay."

I slapped between her legs. She let out an *unf* and curled her feet around my calves.

"When you come," I said in her ear, my hand circling her clit, "Greyson's going to come back."

"I know."

"When you're back in the darkness, I don't want you to worry. I love you."

"And her?"

I wrapped my arm around her so she couldn't move and slapped her cunt again. She tried to twist, but I held her. "And her. All of you."

"You promised her something. Oh, God, that feels so good."

"I promised to fuck your ass. But I didn't say when."

"What about now?"

I hadn't expected that. I'd thought she was making sure I wouldn't. But with her head on my shoulder and her legs spread over me, she was looking at me hopefully. Maybe she saw my hesitation. Maybe she was just impatient. She pulled my restraining arm away and got up to face me. Her hair was a sexy mess, and her tits were pink where I'd abused them.

The thought of her tightest hole made me hard again. "Get on the bed."

She went the few steps to the bed and bent over it with her ass up. "Like this?"

"For now."

I walked to the bathroom, stripping clothes as I went. I grabbed lubricant and brought it back to the bed.

"This ass." I kissed it.

Laying her cheek on the sheets, she smiled at me. "You like it?"

I gave her a slap. "I love it."

Dropping the lotion at the top of her crack, I positioned myself against her cunt.

"First this." I entered her easily and pushed the lotion to her anus, massaging it until it accepted my finger. She gasped. "You all right?"

"Yes."

"Do you remember me doing this to you?"

"I think. Everything's foggy."

Was she close to coming back? Was this a sign? Would she be whole or another split?

"What do you remember?"

She paused, bending her head so she could pull her hair over one shoulder. "It hurts at first."

"I'm going to keep that to a minimum." Two fingers, slowly. She cringed. "Try to relax. Trust me." When they were all the way in, I twisted them to loosen her. The cringe slackened to something more like pleasure. "That's my girl." Pulling out, I gave her bottom a light slap. "On your back."

She rolled over. I spread her legs, bending her knees until I could see her wet cunt and her lubed, relaxed ass. I put her hand on her clit. She hesitated.

"Touch yourself. Bring her back with your own hand."

She pressed her fingers against herself.

I ran the head of my cock along her seam and pressed it against her asshole. "You okay?"

"Yes."

"I'm going to go slow."

"Don't. Do it to me like you do it to her."

I couldn't. I didn't think she could take it without preamble or tease. I'd already given her more warm-up than usual, and she'd need more. But if she was asking for rougher, I could give it.

The head went in.

"Ah!"

"Say stop if—"

"Harder." She rubbed her clit, nodding. "Hurt me."

Yes. Greyson was coming through. I believed it through all evidence to the contrary. Maybe that was a mistake. But I trusted her and leveraged myself against the floor with my knuckles braced against the mattress on either side of her head.

She nodded.

Her consent blinded me with lust so hot I couldn't break it down into its component parts. I drove the entire length of my cock into her ass, and she screamed so loud I stopped.

"Don't stop!"

Fuck it. I pounded her ass like a train without brakes, my face close to hers, belly to belly as she whispered with each thrust.

"Hurt me, hurt me, hurt me."

I wanted to rip her apart. Break her. She scratched my back with both hands.

"So tight," I grunted.

"Hurt it. Harder. Hurt me. I deserve it."

The train had brakes, and those last three words pulled them so hard I screeched to a halt, pulling out of her with my balls ready to burst.

"What did you just say?"

Chapter Nineteen

RESPITE

"What did you just say?"

Caden was bent over me, sweating with strain, teeth gritted. I was clutching his back. My ass felt a strange, distended ache the diameter of his dick.

"Harder. I said—"

"You said you deserved it. Pain."

I didn't deny it, because I did deserve it. I punched his chest, but he didn't reenter me. "Why did you stop?"

"Because I'm not here to give you what you deserve. I'm here to give you what you *like*."

"What's the difference?"

He stood up and sliced the air with his hand. "That's my fucking limit, okay? I can't do that to you." He scanned the floor for his clothes and found his pants. "I love you. I'll do anything for you." He stepped into a leg. "Anything *for* you. But I won't do anything *to* you."

"You have to."

"No, I can't. I can't do this alone. I'll get you off and

back to Greyson, but I'm not judge, jury, and executioner, and I'm not hurting you because you came when he assaulted you. That was your body doing what it was asked to do. It doesn't mean you consented, and it doesn't mean you should be punished."

I needed to be punished, but he was misunderstanding.

"Not for that," I said, though I wasn't sure what I needed to hurt for. "I didn't want to hurt for that."

His embrace was so quick I didn't see him coming. His arms were around, me and his voice was close. He was freshly ground coffee and rich soil. He was at the end of a long tunnel of clarity that was disorganized chaos at the edges. A vignette of nonsense sounds and thoughts closed in on me.

"Why do you think you need to be punished?" By the time he got to "punished," the tiny circle of lucidity was a pinpoint of light.

"I don't know."

"Tell me."

"I can't see it."

"Tell yourself."

"Can we bring her back?" I whined. "I'm so tired."

He took my hands like he'd done a hundred times before, as if he wanted to drill what he was saying into me. "Finish it."

God. He knew. Start to finish, without me telling him, he saw into the tunnel and knew I'd stopped that memory on the roof at the orgasm.

"I can't," I cried. "It's too long. I'm going to break."

"I'll hold you together."

"I need relief. I feel it coming, but I don't know when."

"When you finish, I'll bring her back."

He kissed my knuckles. The sunlight came diffuse through the blinds, hitting the blue in his eyes. The irises looked like blue glass bowls. They covered me and only me. A sky of my very own, watching me, protecting me, pinning me to the security of the earth.

I crumpled into his arms, whispering a lie I didn't expect him to believe, shaking the last of my denial out of the bottom of my mind.

"It's finished. I swear."

Caden didn't press, harangue, or demand I tell the truth. He sat on a chair, draping me over his lap, and held me. He accepted that whatever the next part of this memory was, he would be the sky over me.

I knew why Greyson loved him because I fell in love with him too.

As the feel of Caden stroking my hair fell into the background, the gears churned back to life. I was on the roof again, with ripped tights and a throbbing clit.

THE ORGASM WAS STILL hot between my legs.

The guy in the chambray shirt leaned heavy on my body with a look of surprised satisfaction. "You hot little slut."

Without thinking, I landed a hard clap on his face. "Get off me!"

"That's how you want it?" He slapped me.

I touched my face in horror. That wasn't how I wanted it. Not at all. But he thought so, and he pushed me down with one hand and reached for his dick with the other. In a moment of imbalance, I rolled and got out from under him, crawling away while he got on his feet.

"No!" Swaying, blood dripping down my leg, I got my feet under me, feeling everything as if I'd been abandoned by the numbing of the eighth kamikaze.

"Fuck you," he growled. "You came. The least you can do is suck me off."

"If I suck your dick, I'm going to throw up."

That wasn't an idle threat. My stomach was eager to expel what felt like half a gallon of vodka and triple sec. He must have known it. His tone changed back to the guy I'd kind of liked for a couple of hours.

"Come on." He came a step closer. I took half a step back. "Hand job. You already touched it. Don't leave me hanging. It's going to hurt like hell if you do."

"I'm sorry. I just... I'm not ready."

He held out a hand for me and saw the blood on his fingers. "Man, I busted your cherry?"

"It's okay," I said. "Not a big deal."

"Fuck." He was staring at his fingers.

I walked toward him a little, thinking he felt guilt. I was foolish.

"I bet you're so tight."

Was that supposed to be a compliment? I couldn't tell.

"Listen," he said as if he was the most reasonable guy on the planet, "it's busted. You might as well. You came already."

His cajoling tone made me very, very angry. Rage filled me like a foul, sulfuric burn.

"You mean like a hot little slut?"

"That wasn't an insult."

"Like fuck it wasn't." I stepped forward, and he took half a step back. "You put your fingers where I didn't want them."

"You seemed to like it." Defensive. Irritated.

I should have been worried he'd come at me again, but his moment had passed. This was a guy who didn't think of himself as a rapist even when he raped.

"I. Said. No."

"But you *came.*" He put his dick back in his pants and zipped up. "If you don't appreciate what I just did for you, then fuck you."

I hated my orgasm because it made me into a liar. It made me into a prude who—deep down—wanted it. It made me into a cocktease. It made him *right.*

"I'm sorry."

What was I apologizing for?

I'd said no, but I'd come right onto his hand.

He offered a slice, and I'd taken the whole pie.

I was too drunk, too young, too fragile to know I didn't owe him an apology. But he was shrewd. If I was drunk, young, and fragile enough to apologize, maybe the night wasn't over.

"It's all right," he said, using his forgiveness to take a step closer. "Did it feel good?"

He asked as if he was curious, not as if he wanted to weaponize the answer.

"Yeah." I shrugged. "Thank you."

He reached for me, and I let him move the fall of hair away from my eye. "You're really pretty when you're mad."

"Thanks. We should—"

—go.

I never got to finish the sentence. He was on me. Trying to push me down. He was going to take what he wanted no matter what I did.

Once I was down, I was done. I knew that much.

There wasn't a middle ground. I had to resist all the way or not at all.

My anger coalesced into a fine laser of energy, a force directed squarely at his chest, propelling me forward with all my weight. I pushed him not just away, but back so hard he stumbled with one leg crossing over the other, losing his balance until his calf hit the ledge and he disappeared over the edge.

IN THE MIDDLE space between the mind and the world outside it, I watched the shape of his body change as he fell over, the expression on his face. The second before I heard the *hssp* of a one-hundred-seventy-pound sack of bone and tissue hit the ground lasted a lifetime.

In the hours/minutes/seconds between that sound and the sight of his body on the ground, bent like a swastika with his head in a pillow of black blood, I went cold. Everything emptied out of me. Every emotion, thought, personality trait spilled out as if a bucket had been shot full of holes.

And while it all emptied out, another orgasm filled me. This one was real, given not taken, meant to heal instead of break.

It would be my last.

My last as me.

The memory had been found. The dark place touched. I had no more secrets from myself.

As the pleasure opened, I collapsed into the same shape I'd been in when I was released. I'd snap back into Greyson the way I had before but aware of how I was folded and how I fit.

When I came, she came, and when I went back into my place, something else cracked inside her.

Us.

Me.

The thing on the other side of the crack was cold, calculating, deadly.

It took my place in the darkness. It was only a matter of time before it got out.

And then, with nowhere else to go, I went home.

Chapter Twenty

GREYSON

Pleasure held hands with pain as a soul-emptying orgasm ripped through me. I felt as if I didn't have a body at all except for the place where his tongue met my clit and his hand twisted the soft skin of my thigh.

When I opened my eyes to the ceiling of my studio in the Green Zone, I felt reborn. My husband's gentle tongue left my body, and I loosened my grip on his hair.

"Grey?" he said from below. "Baby?"

"I remember."

"Are you all right?"

"Caden." When I said his name, I felt that part of me that had cracked off and shaken loose. It rattled like a car part that would need replacing. It would drop out of the chassis in the driveway or going eighty on the freeway.

He crawled up until his body was a bridge over mine, eyes flicking over my face as if gathering data. "Are you whole? That's what I'm really asking. Is it over?"

His eyes were the blue of the Iraqi sky, with all its

promise of comfort and spectacle of power. I ran my fingers over his jaw and neck as if for the first time. I didn't want to disappoint him, but I didn't want to lie either. "No."

He bowed his head, cutting me off from him and his protection.

"I'm so sorry for what I did," I said.

"I know."

"I killed him."

"It was self-defense." He kissed my cheek as if that made it any better.

"And then I sent my brother to clean off his fingers. That wasn't self-defense. That was a crime."

"That was his choice."

"Caden, I wanted to turn myself in but…"

"But Jake. You did the right thing. Your brother protected you, and you protected him."

He was right, but he was wrong. Where law met order, he was dead wrong, but where the burden was shared, he was right. God damn him, and God damn me. I didn't know how to live with this.

"It was wrong," I said. "He was somebody's son, and it was *wrong*."

"We can dissect this later," he said, sitting up. "They're coming for you soon."

"Who?" I got up on my elbows.

"Blackthorne. They're working on a treatment for this in Saudi." He got up. When the mattress went flat, I felt the abandonment of his weight. "They want you to go."

"What treatment? What is it? Behavioral? Occupational? Clinical? What are we dealing with here?"

"I don't know. I don't know a damned thing. I didn't know which questions to ask, and I still don't. I don't trust him or the company he works for, but there's no one else and nothing else unless we're going to recreate you killing someone and making a different decision. Or gaining control of it. Or whatever it's going to take. I'm not willing to do that."

He looked lost. I didn't often see him in the space between knowing who he was and making a decision, where the variables weren't organized and the choices led to unknown ends. It was from this crack that Damon had gathered his traits.

"What if I don't want to go?"

"Then you don't go."

I got off the bed. "Then I'm not going. There. Done." I stepped into my clothes. "We stay together and figure it out together."

"There's a problem."

"We'll figure it out." I buttoned my pants as if I was punctuating a sentence.

"I'm AWOL. We're not going to be together much longer."

My loose, cracked-off part rattled. It spoke to me by freezing and hardening my decision into a solid mass, breaking it off until it wasn't a decision anymore. It was an old thing that didn't work. I was left with a cold calculation from a dangerous piece of myself...

Let him go.

... and a hot need directed outward, at him...

He cannot go.

"How long?" I asked, hoping to settle the tug-of-war inside me.

"Too long. Way too long."

"Jesus Christ on a ladder, Caden. What were you thinking? Have you talked to anyone? Have they issued a warrant? Are the MPs coming?"

He didn't have to answer. All he had to do was look away, and I knew.

Let him go.

He cannot go.

I cracked again. His forgiveness and unconditional love were the only things gluing me together. I cracked harder than he had after Damon slipped away.

"Grey." He was near me, on me, holding me up as my legs lost the ability to keep me standing. "Grey. It's going to be all right."

Let him go.

He cannot go.

The decision wasn't rhetorical. Coldly, I didn't care if we separated, but if we separated, I was sure I'd die. If I chose, I'd be rent in two again. It took all my concentration to exist between the two choices, leaning in both directions and neither.

Let him go.

He cannot go.

Once I chose, I'd split, and one side would show herself while the other got locked in a bag. I knew this like I knew I had two feet and ten fingers, because I was sane and that sane part of myself could see it all happening but was helpless to do anything about it.

Let him go.

He cannot go.

"Baby, listen." He was on his knees with me, crouched between the erect and the supine, keeping me from complete surrender. "I'll go with you. Both of us to Saudi. They won't separate us. Come back. Come back to me."

He turned my face to his. He was so strong. He'd decide. All I had to do was follow, and I'd hold together.

"I can't take this anymore," I said. "I can't live like this."

Far, far away, there was a knock on the door.

"You can, and you will. Do you hear me?"

The way he ignored the knocking and focused on me and me alone gave me the strength to hold the pieces of myself together. "I hear you."

He helped me up after another, more urgent, knock. "Are you ready?"

"Stay with me."

"I'm with you, baby. I'm always with you."

He reached out to answer the door. I grabbed his arm. "What if it's the MPs?"

He paused, arm around me, close enough to feel his heart beat.

"I love you," he said, and while still holding me, he opened the door and sunlight flooded in.

Chapter Twenty-One

CADEN

The Suburban's windows were tinted so black they were nearly opaque, dimming the Middle Eastern morning into a dull twilight. Thank God, because a Humvee with MP spray-painted on the side passed in the opposite direction, engine roaring.

Ronin wasn't in the car. He was meeting us at the landing pad. The driver was a bald white guy built like a bookcase. In the passenger seat sat a Latina with her hair twisted into a biscuit at the base of her neck. They wore charcoal-colored Kevlar and had spiral wires looped from their back collars to buds tucked in their ears.

"You all right back there?" the white guy asked, making eye contact in the rearview.

"Yeah." I had my arm around Greyson.

She was looking straight ahead. The look wasn't like Respite's middle-distance stare, which was a passive gaze inward. This was a look of deep, scalpel-sharp concentration.

"Should be eight minutes to the chopper," the Latina said. "Hopefully you'll be in the air before they catch up."

And if not?

If we got held up at a checkpoint? Blackthorne might intervene for Greyson, but I'd be hauled off for a well-earned court-martial. Our separation would break my wife's heart, and like a virus of despair, mine would follow.

"It's okay," I whispered to her. "It's all okay. I have this. I have your back."

We hit a pothole, and her head bounced a little. It could have been a nod, or I could have been losing her second by second.

IN FRONT of a six-story Blackthorne building not far from my wife's old office, I held my hand out, wondering if I'd have to carry her, but she took it and slid down to the pavement.

"Can you walk?" I asked quietly.

"Hold my hand."

She didn't have to ask. I had no intention of letting her go.

A phalanx of Kevlar vests and curly earpieces surrounded us. Six of them, armed to the teeth, led us into the building, through the marble-and-brass lobby built to show the opulence of an oil-rich country. We were hustled into a plexiglass elevator. Even though they surrounded us so we couldn't be seen from the street,

Greyson squeezed my hand hard enough to hurt. Heights. Her least favorite thing. Maybe because of her fall from a diving platform, but maybe because of the boy at the Red Spot. Falling and dying had been a buried reality for her for a long time, manifesting as the most rational of irrational terrors.

The walls of the top floor rattled, and when one of the guards slapped open the door to the roof, I heard the reason for the shakiness in the *thup-thup-thup* of a chopper.

Greyson and I climbed together, side by side, my arm tightly around her to let her know I was there. I wasn't leaving. I would hold her up until the world forced us apart. Until there were no more options. Until they took me away kicking and screaming. Until death did us part.

Ronin stood by the open door of the helicopter with his head turned away from us. His profile was somehow so deliberate I had to question it for a moment, then when he waved without turning, I knew. He was trying to not look at Greyson. He knew she made him change.

The noise of whooping air beat my ears, but as we crossed the roof, the sound of sirens cut through. The ledge around the roof was low enough to let me recognize the Humvees by their speed and the MPs spray-painted on the roofs. They raced away from Greyson's part of the Green Zone right toward us.

We were going to make it, yet I was frozen in place.

I knew how long it took a chopper to get off the ground. I recognized the building I was on. I knew its placement in the Zone. We were going to make it before the cars got to us. She and I would go to a Blackthorne site where a cure might wait. We'd be together.

It was all going to work out.

Ronin stood by the open door, hands in his pockets, gaze averted, wind whipping his hair into a nest.

I'd be a fugitive, and my wife would be in an institution in Saudi Arabia.

But we'd be together.

Right?

She started for the chopper, slipping from under my arm. I grabbed her hand, and she snapped out of the controlled mental effort she'd been making. She looked at me without asking the questions I saw all over her face.

We'd pushed this as far as it was going to go. We'd arrived at a destination. The end of the line. We were at the boundary of our ability to control our fate.

And yet, looking over the edge of the roof to the street below, I had a chance to push harder. I didn't want to, but I had to.

Greyson would have, and she deserved someone at least as resolute as she was.

"Come on!" Ronin called, looking directly at us for the first time.

My wife never accepted a boundary. She'd have pushed a mountain across the desert for me. She wouldn't give up when she saw a wall. She'd break it down, dig under it, climb over it, and conquer whatever was on the other side.

"I love you," I said, the roar of the Humvees getting closer. "I'd marry you again."

"Okay?"

The question at the end of a statement. Respite. The part of her personality that looked to the past for answers wanted to know why I had to tell her I'd marry her again.

"You're everything, Greyson. My life with you is all I have. But the only way to protect you is to let you go."

"Wait." She shook her head quickly, as if getting the bees out of her ears. "No."

"They'll chase me, and if they find me, they'll find you. It'll be ten times worse."

"Let's *go*!" someone shouted.

I took a big step backward, until my heel was on the two-foot-high ledge of the roof. She put her arms around me, clamping me in the cage of her body.

"No!" She looked up at me, pleading.

I wasn't sure I could go through with this, yet I had to do it. I had to detach myself, cut her open, and watch her heart beat before it broke.

"I'm sorry!" I reached behind and pulled her hands away.

She did exactly what I'd expected, clinging harder, pushing into me, trying to wrap her legs around me. "Don't you do it! Don't you leave me!"

Our bodies twisted together in a push and pull. A locking of limbs and muscle. I took her by the wrists, fingers pressed to the scars inside them.

Over her shoulder, Ronin was jogging toward us.

Shit. Time to push.

I let her arms go.

"I have to," I said coldly, calling on the surgeon and the sadist to do the speaking for me. "You have to go alone."

"You promised."

"I had to get you here." I shrugged.

Her face darkened from desperation to rage. Betrayed. Abandoned. Lied to. With eyes afire and hair whipping around her, she was beautiful and terrifying. Pure power and splendor.

"Grey!" Ronin said, three steps from us.

She grabbed my arms, and I tried to pull her off, but she didn't budge. The Humvees stopped at the street below, six stories down and one step backward.

"Good-bye, baby."

I yanked my arms away, and she pushed me, trying to stay connected but also showing me her anger. She pushed too hard. I lost my balance, knees cut to bending by the ledge, and let her go so I wouldn't pull her over the edge with me.

What I let go of, she grabbed for, catching my shirt, clamping onto it hard as if she had the strength to pull me back.

Which she didn't.

My weight pulled her over.

We were in the air, the beating of the chopper blades snuffed out by the wind in my ears, grounded by neither earth nor the safety of a cable.

Free floating.

Subject to the single-minded will of gravity.

We spilled down.

A second lasted forever in frightening lucidity. The blue of the sky. The smell of sand and gas in the air.

She was next to me and a little above, hair flying back,

one shoe lost to wind shear, fingers shaped into hooks as she reached for me.

What gravity pulled down, the wind pushed up. My hand reached for hers, and we touched, sliding our palms together in the split moment before impact.

Chapter Twenty-Two

GREYSON

Lucidity wasn't always sanity. Illusions often seemed clear and reasonable.

That may be the very definition of insanity. Not that a mind was muddled or confused, but that it was too clear and concise when facing its own misrepresentations, without the ability to turn to reality. Not without help.

Which was to say, everything got clear on the way down. My life was a deck of cards being bent from the bottom and shuffled. I could see the face cards flipping by, each one an event in my life.

A person who touched me. Events, meaningless and otherwise. A thing I saw once.

Lia, who shows me how to make the Egyptian points on the corners of my eyes.

Jake, who yells when I break his Walkman.

July Fourth barbecue. The smell of chlorine and ketchup. Colin drinks a beer. He has Dad's chin.

My sixth birthday. I'm at the head of the table. I pretend I am queen.

The *thup-thup* of hundreds of helicopter rotors.

In the backseat, the way the sun bursts over the line of the mountains while my brothers argue.

A clown on stilts hands out bananas.

My mother at the kitchen table, doing a crossword. And Caden.

Half-seen in slow motion as we parted on the way down—I wouldn't let him fall alone. Not this time.

Caden.

Whose love woke me so slowly I didn't realize I'd been sleeping.

Whose body was the source of my deepest aching need.

Whose arms shook as he carried me to the CSH in Balad. The sun peeking from behind him, bursting as if he was my horizon line.

Whose body was life.

Who opened the mail with a rip and a blow.

Who never let me fall until I pushed him.

Whose eyes held the promise and protection of the sky above.

Caden.

Who was suspended in the air next to me, his posture a scribble of unlikely angles, released from the constraint of gravity even as he was imprisoned by it.

He was reaching for me, and I didn't have to abandon him.

I couldn't save us, but I'd tried. I'd grabbed his shirt

and tried to pull him back. Physics and inertia sent me over with him, but I wasn't an observer to my foolishness.

I'd tried.

Time stretched. All was still. The pressure of the air under me was leverage enough to reach for him. Touch him. Hand to hand. Skin on skin. I had him.

I was so sorry. Wrecked with a regret I'd never have time to process.

But I'd tried.

Everything was clear.

And real.

Clicking into place—Forgiveness matched with responsibility. Sorrow with hope. Contentment with worry. Death with love. Acceptance with elation.

Caden with Greyson.

The complete puzzle came together, and clarity matched with reality.

Which is to say, I knew I was going to die sane.

Chapter Twenty-Three

CADEN

SAN DIEGO
OCTOBER, 2005

I hadn't thought I'd ever get married. I didn't love bachelorhood or despise the institution of marriage. It wasn't a position I'd staked out and defended. It was simpler than that. I'd long ago accepted the fact that I was emotionally unqualified for the job of husband.

Then she'd come, and it didn't matter.

Nothing else mattered. Not my rented tux or the wedding gown she'd plucked off the rack like a pair of jeans. Not Doug, the photographer who worked for the local paper. Not the brown sludge seeping into the hem of her dress or the grit between my toes.

What mattered was the sun setting behind her, the way her laughter rose above the bang and gurgle of the crashing waves, the wind pulling her veil behind her toward the infinite ocean.

She was connected to the sun, the sea, the wind, and the sand, and I was connected to her.

I'd never thought I'd get married, but how could I have known a woman like her existed?

"Stop kissing for one minute, guys!" the photographer cried. "I can't see your faces."

I opened my eyes. She had sand in her lashes.

"We should let the man do his job," I said.

"If we wanted posed pictures, we would have hired that other lady."

I turned to Doug and smiled, keeping her close. Behind him, her parents watched. Dad held Mom's shoes. Jake and Colin were to the right, still arguing about politics as a cover for deep personality differences. Cousins, uncles, aunts, none mine before this day, played in the sand or wrinkled their noses at their sullied finery.

I heard the hiss of the foaming wave before I felt the cold rush on my feet, and as Greyson squealed, I sank an inch into wet sand and laughed. Doug *click-clicked*, and we ignored him.

"I just lost the deposit on this tux."

She picked up the skirt of her dress. "It's ruined," she laughed. "I guess I can't wear it again."

I swept her in my arms and spun her. "I'll shred it later just to make sure."

"Oh no!" she cried when I put her down. "Look!"

Five feet away, a sand castle was getting waterlogged.

"Let's move out," Dad called. "The caterer's going to start in half an hour."

"We have thirty minutes to save it!" Veil dragging, she

ran to the castle. "Mom!" She tossed her mother her shoes.

"Twenty minutes," I said. "Ten minutes to drive back."

She got on her knees and patted the base of the castle. "Help me!"

"You can't be serious?"

Looking up at me with a streak of sand on her left cheek and the last bits of the sun catching the hairs flying out of her up-do, she caught me in the web of her higher expectations.

I got on my knees across from her, the castle between us.

"Just this one thing." She pointed at a tower that had survived the wave. It had been made by a careful child, with evenly cut turrets and a window with sticks for bars.

"Hurry." I got my hands under it, and she did the same.

A wave smashed and foamed, ripping toward us as we carefully lifted the tower without a second to spare.

"Slowly," I said. "Careful."

"Okay. We got it."

Doug took his pictures. Jake and Colin stopped arguing. The kids watched with wide eyes. Everyone held their breath, rooting for us to move the tower to safety.

We stepped over the newly wet sand, balancing the piece of the castle. With every step, the tower cracked and split, and as we stepped out of the tidal zone, it collapsed in our hands.

A collective *aww* went up.

"We tried," I said, slapping the sand off my hands.

She looped her arm through mine. "We did."

When I kissed her, she tasted like sea foam, so I kissed her again and again on the way back to the house.

We tried.

We did.

Epilogue

CADEN

Death changes you even when you don't die.

I'd recognized the Blackthorne building as soon as we got to the roof, and I saw the yellow-and-blue striped airbag below. I had a second to decide if the opportunity to have Greyson push me off a building would occur. I didn't have time to ask if the bag was inflated or if it was safe. I didn't have time to train in the proper way to fall.

If I'd had a second more to think about it, I wouldn't have put her at risk.

Maybe I just did impulsive things when she was about to get on a helicopter with Ronin. Maybe I'd never know, and maybe it would never matter.

The bag had been inflated, and we fell side by side. Not quite safely, but not quite dead either.

"Baby!" I wrestled the inflated bag to turn to her.

"Caden!"

Anything could be wrong. I hadn't seen the angle of

her fall, and it took very little to paralyze a person from that height.

"Can you feel your hands and feet?"

"Yes." The sound of her voice was a song, and her expression was sharp and aware. "Are you—?"

"I'm fine."

I rolled on top of her, pushed by the movement of the air in the bag. Four hands clasped between our chests.

"We're fine," I said.

"We're fine."

I was promptly arrested.

DEATH CHANGES you even when you don't die.

I was court-martialed, demoted, and had my bonus taken. It wasn't fun. I stated my case, expressed regret, took responsibility, but also made it clear that I would always do what I had to do to save my wife. Greyson was a character witness, as were her father and Jake, whose survival after capture was a miracle. Ronin testified with eyes averted from my wife's face.

What kept me going through the shame of it all was Greyson. She was whole. We'd recreated her pivotal moment, and she'd taken control of it the way I'd taken control of my own.

That was the only cure so far.

By the time I was a free man, Blackthorne had quietly ended the BiCam study. They'd shuttered the medical study division, wiping it from their website as if it had never existed. Ronin went into the Saudi facility. I hoped they found a simpler cure, but knew they'd never tell me.

In the end, I was treated fairly. I negotiated staying in the army even after I could have been discharged. Greyson didn't admit to wanting to keep her connection to the military, but I knew she did. Once she told me she was pregnant, I knew I had to stay.

DEATH CHANGES you even when you don't die.

I surfed. A few months to forty-two years old, army captain, New York City born and raised, I'd taken up surfing at five in the morning before I had to report at the Presidio.

Monterey was on the wrong side of dawn. The sky over the water didn't change from dark to light as much as it went from navy to cadet, and when the ocean swelled, it looked like a black plastic bag being shaken out.

The surfer rides between the shore and a force that threatens to throw him against it. The push is stronger than any one man, and riding it means using it, respecting it, knowing it can pick you up and slam you against the earth if you're not careful.

Which it did. A lot.

I spun in the brine, tucking my body into itself as I was rolled against the sand and spit up onto the beach with grit between the edges of my suit and my skin.

Shaking out my hair, I located my board and tucked it

under my arm. My watch said I had time for another shot at it and—

"Caden!"

Sun rising behind her, Greyson was pulled forward by our son. He was named Hank, but we called him Yank because he pulled us in all directions as hard as his eighteen-month-old body could. I stuck the board in the sand and held my arms out for the baby. The fat, brown curls he got from my side of the family had been bleached blond by the sun, and the dark eyes he got from my wife were big with delight when I picked him up.

"You're up," I said facetiously.

Of course she was up. Hank didn't actually sleep. It was unusual for her to drive to the beach before seven in the morning. I kissed her, but her lips were tight.

I turned to Hank. "What's Mommy mad about?"

He reached over my shoulder to the bright-yellow board. I put him down.

"I'm not mad," she said.

"Boo!" Hank peered around the board and popped back behind it.

Distracted, I chased him around the yellow barrier. "I'm going to get you!"

Crouching, chasing him in circles as he squealed, I was low enough to see what Greyson had in her hand. A white letter-sized envelope.

Snatching up Hank, I laid him over my shoulder and blew noisy air onto his belly, then I turned him upside down while he laughed and brushed the sand with his fingertips.

"What do you have there, baby?"

She held up the envelope. The front had the US Army seal. "Are you deploying?"

Since I was normal active duty, I would have known weeks ago if I was being sent overseas. Greyson knew that, but once burned, she assumed everything was fire.

Gently, I lowered Hank onto the beach. "No. It's not that."

"What is it then? Why didn't you open it?"

"Because." I snapped away the envelope. "I know what it is, so there's no point." I jammed my finger under the flap's corner and yanked, making a mess of the tear. "And you've been with patients, or I've been on shift. We're busy." I blew into the split to open it. "I was waiting for the right time."

Hank was pulling at my legs to get up.

I held the envelope out to him. "Pull that out."

I had to get it removed halfway before he could get the paper loose. I handed it to Greyson still folded. She took it suspiciously, as if I'd lie about being deployed.

No. She trusted me. She still thought the army could lie, and I didn't blame her.

"Open it," I chided, picking up Hank again.

She swung her head to let the wind keep the hair out of her face and unfolded the page, glancing at me as if to ask if I had anything else to say before I was proven wrong.

"Mommy is a suspicious lady."

Hank made a farting noise with his lips.

Greyson read the letter, every word of it, a satisfied smile growing across her face. "Major St. John. Congratulations."

"I'm off square one."

Her hands dropped, wrinkling the letter. "God, when can I stop worrying about this?"

I reached for her and pulled her close. Hank transferred his weight from me to her. "This is our life, baby. Is it that bad?"

"No. It's perfect."

I kissed Hank's cheek, then her lips. They yielded this time, and I tasted her mouth until Hank jammed his fingers between us, laughing.

"Hanky," I said, "are you ready for your little sister?"

"Yes!" He pointed at his mother's belly, which was just starting to show.

"All right." I gave him to Greyson and picked up my board. "So am I."

"So am I," Greyson said when I took her hand.

Hank wiggled to the ground and pulled us away from the ocean to the car, our home, our life together with its ups, its downs, its surprises and routines.

I helped Greyson onto the curb even though she didn't need it and kissed her until our son pulled her away. I watched her stuttering walk to her car as she tried to keep up with a child who wanted to see everything every minute and wanted to take us along for the ride.

She glanced back at me, smiling, and waved me forward. "Keep up, Major!"

I hitched my board under my arm and chased my family home.

Was our life perfect?

Yes.

Yes, it was.

Epilogue

GREYSON

How many possible futures did I have?

When we walked away from that air bag, I knew I was starting a possible future so unlikely that I needed to appreciate every minute of it.

When I found that envelope, I thought I was coming to another pivot point. A fork in the road where choices had to be made, because I promised myself that if he deployed, we were going with him, logistics and common sense be damned.

"You really dodged a bullet there," I said from the passenger seat. The front of the yellow surfboard stuck out from the roof like a giant duck's bill in the windshield.

"How's that?"

With the windows open, the cool morning air whipped his hair every which way. I'd married a man who was rigid and yoked by darkness, but my husband had a burden-free spirit.

"I was going to take Hank wherever they sent you."

He laughed and put his hand in my lap, twining it with mine.

"Don't ever change, Grey. Never."

"Don't ever leave me. *Ever*."

Hank made little boy sounds in the back, holding a toy helicopter against the window so the sky would be a backdrop.

"I got an email from Ronin," I said.

"Which Ronin?"

"That's the news. There's only one. They used the visualization procedure."

"Yours?" He stopped at a light and turned to me, brows raised. Big smile. God, this man was beautiful when he was happy. "The one you developed?"

"Yup."

He slammed the car into park and put his arms around me. His kiss was insistent and jubilant, made through a smile. He pulled away.

"I'm proud of you."

"I'm pretty proud of myself."

His eyes left mine for a second and he pushed the neckline of my shirt aside, exposing the mark he'd left on me the night before. It was sore to the touch. He was still good at hurting me just enough.

"You better have a doctor look at that," he said.

"Good idea."

"G'een, g'een!" Hank shouted from behind me, kicking my seat. A horn honked behind us.

"Let's go!" Caden said, looking at Hank in the rearview as he crossed the intersection.

"Let go!" his son repeated.

"Onward!" I joined in.

"O'wad!"

"Onward," Caden said, taking my hand as he turned onto our block.

Forward we went.

Always forward, with nothing but the earth beneath us, the blue sky above us, and the horizon line before us.

THE END

IF YOU LIKED this book I am 100% sure you'll enjoy the New York Times Bestsellers in the *Games Duet*.

He'll give her a divorce on one condition. Spend 30 days in a remote cottage with him, submitting to his sexual dominance.

She thinks this is his pathetic attempt to save their marriage. She's wrong.

Marriage Games | Separation Games

Text cdreiss to 77948 to get a message when my next mindfuck series is out, starting with Cry Baby, Cry.

FOLLOW ME ON FACEBOOK, Twitter, Instagram, Tumblr or Pinterest.

Join my fan groups on Facebook and Goodreads.

Get on the mailing list for deals, sales, new releases and bonus content - JOIN HERE.

My website is cdreiss.com

Acknowledgments

Thank you, thank you, thank you for joining me on this journey. This series was for you but also for my own soul. It's not often that the id of a writer and the needs of readers are the same, so I cherish this series for that. My goal was to deconstruct a marriage, piece by piece, examine it, and put it back together. It's because of you, my faithful readers, that I was allowed this conceit.

Throughout the writing of this series, Sarah Ferguson and her husband answered stupid questions about the military in sixty seconds or less. Rebecca Yarros was great help for *Cutting Edge* as I set up life in Fallujah. I learned so much I can barely fit it all in my head. These women make their husbands' sacrifices possible. They serve our country as bravely as the men they love, and they are not to be underestimated.

Sarah is also on my PR team, and it's because of her and Jenn Watson that I was allowed time to write. Yes, this thing was a month late, but they held down the fort while I struggled to make this series what I needed it to be.

Fort-holding-down credit also goes to Jean, Serena, and Michelle for their help with my Facebook group. Cameron makes the gorgeous graphics on Instagram and profile pictures. Ashley makes my emails so effing pretty. Anthony keeps the money where it belongs and is amazingly good at being the soothing voice that cuts through the panic. Thank God for all of them.

Chanpreet Singh used her medical training to help figure out what happened in that closet in Fallujah. A lady from my fan group helped me find the right Kurdish phrase for "I'm pregnant." I've searched my Facebook inbox and cannot find her name. If you're there, wonderful lady, message me again so I can place your name here.

Cassie was a goddess and editor of grace, as always. Her staff, especially superbrain Devon B, proofed the series, and can I tell you something? Devon puts the CMoS numbers in the comments. Super sexy.

Lauren Blakely and Laurelin Paige mentor the hell out of me. I can't even begin to list how many times and ways they extract my head from my ass.

I tried to calculate how long Caden's parents were in the air as they fell. With the help of the internet, it should have been a snap. It wasn't. I finally broke down and asked Penny Reid if she knew anyone who could help me calculate it, and she came back with a number in less time than it took to fall from the 101st floor of the World Trade Center circa 2001.

As always, thank you to my readers: The new ones for

taking a chance on a genre-straddling series and the old for sticking with me. I hope I can continue to entertain you for years to come.

———

I took liberties with history, military procedure, and medicine. I've listed them below in the order they occurred to me. There are probably more I'm not aware of. I apologize if any of these took you out of the story.

1. There was no major *shamal* (sandstorm) in Baghdad in 2007. There was one in 2005 and 2008. The May storms are called Al-Haffir or "the driller," which is a fact irrelevant to this list but delightful nonetheless.
2. Surgeons didn't go with medevacs regularly until 2011. Their presence saved lives, but not in 2007.
3. Medical teams worked for eight days straight at the outset of Phantom Fury (the second battle of Fallujah) with minimal rest. I have no evidence they were being given amphetamine or any other performance-enhancing drug.
4. Abu Ghraib was the site of horrible acts of torture I never want to see again. As far as I am able to ascertain, the Department of Defense did not order these specific acts as a way to "use their culture against them." Ronin's quote is an expression of my belief

that people do not act in a vacuum, not point of fact.

5. This one isn't really a fudged fact, but it's worth mentioning. I have done bioenergetic/circular breathing many times. The effects are exactly what's in the book. You should give it a try.

6. The characters' personality problems were the result of an experimental drug that I made up, so the presentation of very real, very serious dissociative disorder wasn't even close to textbook. Mental illnesses, in general, are not as easy to cure as some made up drug side effect in a book. I hope I was clear in that.

7. On capitalization: I know the military has their own style guide, but I don't like it. I follow the Chicago Manual of Style. I don't capitalize army or rank unless I'm specifically talking about the US Army in a formal way or using rank with a person's name. This can get pretty fuzzy in casual prose. When there was even the slightest bit of doubt, I opted to not cap army or rank. The word "soldier" should never be capitalized unless it's the first word in a sentence. It's my book. I do what I want. End.

8. The word "crazy" is only used in context of character. If the character would think or say it, they do. Greyson wouldn't. Caden would (though by book three, he was less dismissive). Mental illness is serious, debilitating, and worthy of compassion and resources. I hope I

dealt with it in a way that expresses reality as well as respect. If you don't think I lived up to my ideals, let me know.

9. Jake's abduction is loosely based on the capture of US military personnel in May 2007. It is not meant to match the historical record or erase the stories of the lives that were lost.

10. Getting these two to jump from a plane/helicopter/building without her knowing she'd live was a puzzle I was putting together, taking apart, and rearranging until the last minute. Seriously. Do those bags just stay inflated all the time? Doesn't someone have to be there to deflate at the point of impact? Six stories? Really? I hope I didn't push credulity too far in this or anything.

\<end\>

The Edge Series

Rough. Edgy. Sexy enough to melt your device.

Cutting Edge | Rough Edge | On The Edge | Broken Edge | Over the Edge

Contemporary Romances

Hollywood and sports romances for the sweet and sexy romantic.

Shuttergirl | Hardball | Bombshell | Bodyguard

Made in the USA
Middletown, DE
22 August 2018